OTHER BOOKS BY
JILL SYLVESTER

YOUNG ADULT FICTION
The Land of Blue
Awakening – Devon: Dream Agent – Book 1

NONFICTION
Trust Your Intuition: 100 Ways to Transform Anxiety and
Depression for Stronger Mental Health

PIECES

JILL SYLVESTER

OLD TREE HOUSE
PUBLISHING

PIECES
BY JILL SYLVESTER

Old Tree House Publishing
Copyright ©2021 Jill Sylvester
All rights reserved.

Old Tree House Publishing
PO Box 462
Hanover, MA 02339

This is a work of fiction. Names, characters, businesses, places, events and incidents are either the products of the author's imagination or used in a fictitious manner. Any resemblance to actual persons, living or dead, or actual events is purely coincidental.

Editor: Rebecca McCarthy, www.thewrittencoach.com
Copyeditor: Jody Amato, jodyamato@gmail.com
Cover and Interior Layout: Yvonne Parks, PearCreative.ca
Proofreader: Clarisa Marcee, www.AvenueCMedia.com
Author Photo: Maura Longueil

Publisher's Cataloging-In-Publication Data
(Prepared by The Donohue Group, Inc.)

Names: Sylvester, Jill, author.
Title: Pieces / Jill Sylvester.
Description: Hanover, MA : Old Tree House Publishing, [2021] | Series: Devon: dream agent ; [2] | Interest age level: 013-018. | Summary: "Seventeen-year-old Devon Alante squinted in the darkness of her bedroom. Even though she couldn't recall many of the details, the message was very clear: Her dreams weren't wrong. Something or someone was letting Devon know for certain that her best friend Gwen's boyfriend, Andrew, wasn't all that he appeared to be ... Then one day, Devon finds her deceased mother's journal and discovers that her mom and her best friend may have something in common. Is her mom the one sending Devon the dreams to try and help Gwen?"--Provided by publisher.
Identifiers: ISBN 9780998977591 (paperback) | ISBN 9781737164609 (Kindle) | ISBN 9781737164616 (ePub)
Subjects: LCSH: Teenage girls--Juvenile fiction. | Dreams--Juvenile fiction. | Diaries--Juvenile fiction. | Best friends--Juvenile fiction. | CYAC: Teenage girls--Fiction. | Dreams--Fiction. | Diaries--Fiction. | Best friends--Fiction.
Classification: LCC PZ7.1.S95 Pi 2021 (print) | LCC PZ7.1.S95 (ebook) | DDC [Fic]--dc23

DEDICATION

To my clients, who continue to do the brave and courageous work it takes to live a full life.

"The general function of dreams is to try to restore our psychological balance by producing dream material that re-establishes, in a subtle way, the total psychic equilibrium."

CARL JUNG

CHAPTER ONE

I wondered if I looked the part. The full-length mirror on the back of the bathroom door swayed and tilted while I stared. Dad never used the glue he said he would in order to keep it secure, *but what else is new?* My small hands trembled as I buttoned the top button of the pale blue sweater I picked out for class. The one I found at the bottom of my bureau drawer—a sweater I forgot I had purchased, for some future event that might require looking like I had it together. I guess tonight fit the bill.

Looking back at my reflection, I thought of how Gram used to refer to me as her "little doe," which had to do with my small size, since my eyes weren't brown—and actually kind of matched my sweater, now that I thought about it. These days, though, the more I thought about *the little doe* reference, I realized that it might have had more to do with the deer-in-the-headlights look I sometimes had, when I would just stand there and kind of freeze, you know, whenever I felt nervous. I guess, given everything from the past, this made a lot more sense than just my being petite.

I definitely saw the deer-in-the-headlights look on my face right now.

I unbuttoned the top button of the sweater, thinking it made me look too stiff that warm night in early May. Matched with a pair of cropped, light denim jeans, courtesy of my best friend Gwen's better fashion sense, it hit me that wearing jeans might not be appropriate, since the workshop at the police station was offered only to adults. Except for me.

I checked the time on my phone.

Ten minutes to go.

Turning sideways to glance at myself, I remembered how Detective Dyer told Dad that no teenager had ever been asked to study along with the other officers. Because of what had happened last fall—my "hits" in the Denise Franklin case—the Hanley Police Department was making an exception.

I felt a pit in my stomach as I thought about how the detectives and cops, and whoever else might be taking the workshop, might view me—probably like an immature high-school kid attending one of their grown-ups-with-real-jobs seminars.

I squeezed the skin on the inside of my arm, under the sweater where you couldn't see if it made a mark. I hoped, no, I *prayed*, I could gain control of this whole intuitive thing. Detective Len had suggested last year that by taking this course, I might be able to.

I stepped closer to the mirror, my reflection clear since Avo had wiped the glass clean the other night when she stopped by to bring supper. My paternal grandmother still made food for us a few nights a week—partly because my grandmother liked to cook and know what was going on in our lives and partly because my father was still reliant on his mother at thirty-five years of age.

I continued to stare at myself, finding more shortcomings, including the sleeves of the sweater being a bit too short. It was my own fault. I hated shopping. I only bought this after Avo gave me a gift card for my birthday freshman year cause I felt like I needed to get something. It wasn't like I could ask Avo to take me to get a professional outfit or whatever for this class. All she wanted to talk about was what I was planning to wear to prom in June and how handsome my father looked back in the day. I didn't have the heart to tell my grandmother that I wasn't planning on going to the stupid prom, since the sophomore dance had been as boring as Mr. Morelli's history lesson on Mesopotamia. I didn't fit in with the kids in high school, but she refused to see the truth.

I wet my fingertips and smoothed my full eyebrows into place, staying true to my un-made up face. In trancelike fashion, the way things often came to me, an image flashed into my mind, of that good looking, rookie cop Bobby Dempsey. I had met him when Len interviewed me at the station about the visions I had regarding Denise's case. I wish I knew whether he was taking the class. If he was, since Len alluded to his being interested in becoming a detective someday, it would kind of make me feel weirdly less nervous—probably because he'd be the only person closest to my age. But then it made me kind of panicky, too, since I was pretty sure Bobby wasn't the least bit interested in an almost seventeen-and-a-half-year-old junior in high school.

I counted the few freckles scattered on my nose that everyone always said looked cute. I guessed it didn't matter whether Bobby was there or not. All I really cared about was doing a good job in this remote viewing intro class—one that could lead to being included in the continuing advanced class if you "showcased skill" to impress the detectives. Especially Len Dyer, and I guess maybe Bobby too, for no other reason than there was no one else in my life I cared to impress—unlike my other friends with their new relationships and happening social agendas.

My cell phone vibrated on the bathroom counter.

A message from Gwen:

"You're going to kill me!"

I tapped the keys quickly with my thumbs: "What's wrong?"

"I know I said I would drive you, but A's giving me a hard time about leaving in the middle of a fight. Can you call Frankie? UGH. I'm SO SORRY."

I bit my lip, hard, not caring for a second whether it bled. Frankie, our other best friend from the neighborhood and, more importantly, my other ride since I didn't have my license yet, was at the gym with his football buddies, according to his most recent Snapchat. There wouldn't be enough time for him to come get me, since class started in fifteen minutes and the police station was five miles away, on the other side of town.

I cursed Gwen and her arrogant, annoying boyfriend Andrew—who Frankie often referred to as the real-life Gaston from *Beauty and the Beast,* since Andrew walked around like every girl in the world wanted him—as I dialed my Dad's number, heavy-footed on my way into the kitchen.

Dad was the last person I wanted to ask for a ride. My father wasn't keen on this whole thing—my dreams and my wanting to develop my intuition.

Three rings. No answer.

I hung up before I heard the raspy tone of Dad's voice mail message, which always sounded more to me like some dating app intro instead of the mature owner of a family business.

I paced the kitchen, my elbow striking the thin *Hanley Times* onto the floor.

Picking it up and tossing it back on the island counter, I realized the only reason we got that stupid paper was because my father liked to keep up on all things Hanley, especially the local sports section. Dad liked to relive his glory days.

I glanced at the microwave clock. Dad was either still at the shop or already out with Tina, his girlfriend of nine months. The longest relationship he ever had outside of my mother. There wasn't time to track him down.

I didn't have the kind of father who might have remembered that class started tonight—the only class I had ever been excited about and had been waiting more than half a year to take. He certainly wouldn't be calling to make sure I had a ride and, God forbid, to wish me luck.

The clock glowed *6:50.*

I cracked my knuckles, trying to remember if Frankie's mom's bike was still stashed out back beside the bulkhead. That wouldn't get me to the station until 7:30, which would make me a half-hour late. The tires could be flat for all I knew; the last time I rode the ten-speed bike was when Frankie, Gwen, and I decided to keep in shape by biking up to the park on Sundays during freshman year. That idea lasted a week.

I heard the birds outside, chirping in that way they do when they're winding down for the night. My breath caught in my throat, scaring me as I felt the familiar feeling of a panic attack coming on. I grabbed my phone and downloaded the Uber app, something I swore I'd never do after everything I'd heard on the news, and booked a ride, wondering how soon a driver could get to my house on Kingston Road in the small, seaside community of Hanley, Massachusetts.

7:15.

I'd get to the station at 7:30, the same time if I had taken the bike. And I had zero guarantees that the Uber driver was normal. My heart raced. That possibility, plus the fact that no one knew I'd booked a ride.

Dad will kill me, I thought, staring as the sun shifted behind the trees in the backyard, *even if he's not here to help me figure out a solution. Shocker.*

I canceled the Uber, kicked off my flats by the front door, and shoved my feet into my sneakers—the black sneakers that most definitely did not go with the outfit Gwen had chosen for me to make a good first impression.

So much for that, I said to myself as I locked the door behind me and prayed that the tires on Janice's bike had enough air.

Thirty-five minutes later, if not for the mud-puddle-filled pothole in front of the newly painted white Hanley town hall from the downpour earlier in the day splashing mud up and across my jeans, sweater, and backpack, I might have arrived at the police station looking halfway decent instead of a disheveled thug.

With my muscles twitching like I was some crack addict, I leaned the bike against one of the budding spruce trees lining the side of the parking lot and sprinted across the blacktop, tripping as I stepped up onto the curb that fronted the concrete building.

I tried to neaten my long, light brown rat's nest of hair reflected back to me in the glass pane of the door. It was no use. I took a deep breath and stepped inside the oak-trimmed foyer. I hoped the woman with the pen in her hand sitting behind the tinted glass window at the back half of the lobby, who felt to me like one of those people who acted like they didn't notice anything but noticed *everything*, didn't witness my less-than-graceful entrance.

While my eyes darted around the foyer, searching for directions to the classroom, a friendly-looking cop with a dimple in his chin approached me in the foyer, asking the nature of my business. It dawned on me that both the cop and the lady behind the glass might be wondering what a teenager was doing at the police station.

Despite the beads of sweat on my forehead and my hair wild around my head, I lifted my chin the way my dad did when he wanted to appear in charge. *Fake it 'til you make it,* he'd say.

I told the officer I was part of the remote viewing workshop for detectives.

"Yeah?" he asked, his thumbs tucked into the waist of his pants.

I nodded, my stomach tying tighter in knots.

The officer sized me up for a moment—*harmless, the word floated into my brain*—and then directed me down the hall toward the conference room.

I politely thanked him and walked down the beige carpet. Outside the closed door of the room, a whiteboard sign in black dry-erase marker read: Parapsychology Research Instructor: Allison Nickerson, Workshop 1: Using Intuition and the Art of Remote Viewing on the Job.

For a moment, I considered leaving. Then, with my heart climbing into my throat the way mercury rises inside one of those old glass thermometers, I turned the silver doorknob.

A blur of men and women, some sporting blue cop uniforms and others wearing regular clothes, glanced at me from four long conference tables that filled the small room like the ones in the Hanley High cafeteria.

The instructor, a really pretty black woman, older, maybe fifty, paused mid-sentence. She reminded me of the way Kerry Washington looked and dressed in *Scandal*—elegant and tailored. She, on the other hand, must have thought I had just emerged from a swamp.

"Nice of you to join us, kid," a bald, overbearing-looking guy with "Walter" written on his white name tag said in a loud voice, making sure everyone else could hear.

My face flushed, made worse, I knew, underneath the florescent lights.

"Millennials," a guy named Ed said under his breath. He wore a mustache like he was stuck in the 80s. "They don't operate on the same clock as everyone else."

It's Generation Z, I thought, standing at the front of the room feeling like a moron. *And yeah, I'm late, but it's not my fault, it's my best friend's because she bailed on me because of her loser boyfriend.* The only words that came out, though, were, "Sorry I'm late."

"You must be Devon," the woman said in an all-business tone. "I'm Allison. Consultant with the Northeastern Research Institute. You can take your seat in the back, please, next to the officer assigned to you."

Now my face burned like I had a fever. Someone was *assigned* to me?

A man raised his hand to identify himself in the third row. The restrained, yet confident smile on his lightly tanned face, with eyes that same blue color of tropical island oceans you find on the Internet. Butterflies burst in my stomach.

Bobby Dempsey.

I made my way to the back of the room and shimmied behind "Hank" to take my seat. Hank, wearing a thick gold rope chain around his equally thick neck—that I instantly knew came from his wife when they first started dating, in that way things came to me when I least expected them—chuckled at the wisecrack remarks taking place at the front of the room.

I sat down in the hard plastic chair beside Bobby—who was even more handsome, and hard-bodied than I remembered—

trying not to fix my hair, which might call even more attention to my less-than-professional appearance.

"I think technically we're classified as Generation Z," Bobby whispered, while he leaned down and adjusted the back of his long, white sneaker.

I laughed under my breath, trying to be cool, trying to show that I wasn't the immature, high school kid they all thought I was, who wouldn't take this class seriously.

If they only knew the truth, I thought after Bobby told me not to mind them, that they were just giving me a hard time. Meanwhile, I had never been more serious about anything in my whole life.

CHAPTER TWO

Two days later, I threw my yellow apron around my waist and started my Saturday afternoon shift at Holly's Ice Cream Barn. Glaring, I watched Gwen in her Lululemon tank top that showed off her naturally toned arms as she carried an uncharacteristically unevenly scooped vanilla ice-cream cone over to the take-out window. A muggy breeze floated in through the mesh screen.

"What's up with you blowing me off like that?" I asked, while Gwen finished making change for her customer. I scraped remnants of Purple Cow ice cream from the middle freezer with more force than usual. "You knew how important that class was to me."

Gwen turned toward me, her eyes puffy and red.

"I'm sorry, okay?" Gwen said. She avoided my gaze, as if she didn't want me to see into her soul. "I messed up your night, and I feel horrible. Don't make me feel worse."

I handed my first customer her small cone while I kept my focus on Gwen. A crumble of ice cream fell on the wrist of the lady's white running jacket.

When the bells jingled on the back of the door, leaving Gwen and me the only ones in the shop, I asked the question I wanted to know the answer to. "What's wrong?"

"Ugh," Gwen said. "Do I need more makeup?" She turned to check her green-eyed, dark-haired self in the muted reflection of the refrigerator.

"No, you don't need makeup," I answered with a sigh. "But seriously, did you really blow me off because your boyfriend told you not to leave in the middle of a fight?"

Checking to see if any customers were approaching the takeout window, Gwen glanced over her shoulder, tanned now that tennis season was in full swing, Turning back to me, she wound the diamond stud in her ear the way she always did when she was upset. "It was mostly my fault. I needed Andrew to understand something. He just won't let stuff go."

I leaned against the counter. "What stuff?"

She shook her head. "Something stupid." She reached for her half-empty, sixteen-ounce Marylou's iced vanilla-something coffee and took a sip. "He got mad when I didn't answer my phone last Saturday night, when we were watching movies at Frankie's. He showed up at my house later and started going off on me. Just in the driveway, but still. Thank God my parents weren't home."

"Why'd he do that?" I asked, my forehead creasing.

Dark colors clouded my mind, like how the sky appears as a storm approaches. Colors tended to show me things, give me messages about situations, about people.

"He just gets jealous," Gwen said. She stared at the floor. "He thought, you know, I was out doing something."

I raised my brow. "You were—you were watching a movie with Frankie and me."

"I know," Gwen said in an exasperated tone, like I didn't understand relationships at all, which of course I didn't, since I hadn't been in one yet, even though I was seventeen and considered pretty. "He thinks I'm out with other guys, that's all."

Three middle-school girls stepped up to the take-out window, giggling as they watched some stupid TikTok video on the brace-faced girl's phone. "But you weren't with other guys, so how could he be mad?" I pushed back the sleeves of my shirt to help Gwen fill the girls' order. She knew I hated making small talk with people and would rather help in the background or clean, if given the choice.

"I told you, it's dumb, I know. Andrew just doesn't want me hanging out with Frankie," Gwen said before handing a dish of ice cream out the window.

"Frankie?" I said, flinching back. "He's like our brother."

"You and I know that," Gwen said, rolling her eyes. "Andrew just thinks his girlfriend should automatically pick up the phone when he calls. Which is why he came to my house and flipped out on me, and I had to calm him down to make sure Mr. and Mrs. Petrucelli weren't watching out the window."

I stared at Gwen in disbelief while she gave the girls their change. "Does Andrew also get mad if you don't pick up at the dinner table?" Gwen's parents had a strict policy of no phones during meals, unlike my father, who basically checked his phone the entire time we ate supper together, which was only a couple times a week these days.

Gwen tossed the fifty-cent tip in the cow container that made a moo sound every time you dropped change into its white-and-black spotted back. "Stop. We're just having an argument, you know, between girlfriend and boyfriend."

I cracked my knuckles while Gwen slid her freshly painted hot-pink nails into a mason jar filled with cream-colored, hard plastic spoons, to retrieve a piece of broken handle.

"Well, sorry you're having an argument, but your 'boyfriend' also owes me an apology."

Gwen closed her eyes tight to block me out, the same way she did when I showed her the loose dress for the sophomore dance that I thought might look good on me last year. She said I needed to "highlight my pretty face and small frame," ultimately picking out something tighter, slinkier, and more fashionable. "Let it go. You can blame it on me. I said I was sorry."

"Whatever," I said, surprised that Gwen took a week to tell me what happened after that night we finally settled on watching *Eighth Grade* at Frankie's. I refused to watch anything in the horror genre since I got enough of that in my dreams. "Does Frankie know he's not on Andrew's favorite person list?"

Gwen shook her head, the doorknob bells sounding in the air. "Speak of the devil."

Frankie strutted up to the counter with his bushy head of hair that made him look a few inches taller than he really was. Gwen said he looked like one of those osprey nests that sit atop skinny telephone poles on Cape Cod. "What up, Bs? Party down the beach tonight on account of the weather *perfection*."

Just then, Holly entered the back door of the shop, peering over her large glasses with the string attached like older ladies seemed to do for whatever reason. "I told you before, Frankie, if you want a job, fill out an application." She swatted him with a dirty dishrag she swiped off the blender counter with one of her thick, mottled hands from too much time spent in the Florida sun during the off-season.

"I'll order something," Frankie mumbled, showing he was still a good kid even though sometimes he acted like a punk. After Holly rearranged the chairs in the parlor and headed past the roped-off area that led into her antique farmhouse, he leaned back over the counter and asked, "You guys in? I assume you will be, G, since your boy lives in the adjacent, though far-less-superior town of Marshton. With no beach rights, I might add, so I don't know why they always think they're included in our Hanley soirees."

"Yeah, I think we're going. Technically, I believe, a soiree is at someone's house and not a beach, though," Gwen said, before heading to the take-out window to wait on the next customer.

"Whatever, AP English. Don't forget your vocab scores weren't as good as mine. Anyhoo, you want to go with me, D? Gwen and Gaston will likely drive their gorgeous selves in a separate, gasoline vehicle." Frankie slapped the counter in a drum roll. "How's that for alliteration? I gotta use that tool in my SAT essays for bonus points."

I straightened the few dollars in the back of the cow container so that they made a perfect rectangle, trying to stop thinking back to when Gwen started making Andrew her priority. "Have we met? You know I'm not into parties," I said. *Especially if Andrew's going,* I wanted to add, but also not wanting to betray Gwen.

Frankie looked up for a second from taking selfies to keep up his Snapchat streaks—a habit he had only recently started, since the three of us had said in middle school we'd never do that to keep up with the in-crowd. "I know that, Miss Introvert, but you'll be with me."

"I'm just going to go home," I sighed, wanting to practice some of the exercises Allison had given us the first night of the workshop. I wanted to make a better impression next Thursday night, since I was certain, as of now, I was probably considered the class joke.

"Actually, I'm not going," Gwen said, tightening her ponytail after she checked her phone. "Andrew said he just wanted to stay in tonight." She wiped whipped cream off two Styrofoam cups in that perfectly neat way she had, and then brought the ice cream sundaes to her customers at the take-out window.

"I bet they're going to do the deed," Frankie mouthed to me. He looked around the shop for Holly's whereabouts.

"Shut up, Frankie," Gwen said, before checking her phone again and then stashing it back under the counter. "We just don't feel like going. It's not a big deal."

I lowered my head to study Gwen's face. *We* or *he* didn't feel like going? The bluntest, most-get-in-your-face person I knew, Gwen never used to be someone who let anyone boss her around. I chewed on my lip. Did things change that much after you had a boyfriend?

———

Later, Frankie drove me home from work, rolling into my gravel driveway. "Thanks," I said, unbuckling my seat belt. "Try not to get into trouble tonight with your new hoodlum friends."

"Don't you worry about me," Frankie said, fixing his hair in the rearview mirror. "I'm more concerned about you, living next to Old Man Coleman."

The light from Mr. Coleman's basement shone through the low-lying bushes, creating shadows on the grass. Old Man Coleman, the name Frankie had given my elderly neighbor back in elementary school when we used to get spooked by how he lived alone after losing his *really* old parents, constantly stared out the window at us like some child molester. Even though Avo and my dad had reassured us numerous times that Mr. Coleman was harmless and had simply gone "bat-shit crazy," Mr. Coleman gave the three of us the creeps.

"Right," I said, grabbing my backpack off the floor.

"Now, I don't want you thinking, while you're home alone and everything, since your dad has more of a social life and gets more action that you do, how Old Man Coleman's down there freezing dead cats he's going to fry up on the stove," Frankie said, chuckling while he changed the radio station, before the song even finished playing. A habitual symptom of his undiagnosed

ADHD, his mom, Janice, always said. Janice was a psych nurse at the hospital and never wanted Frankie on stimulants since his estranged father used to do, and sell, pills.

"Nope, Mr. Coleman likes cats way too much," I said, getting out of the car. "You see the way he feeds those ferals every night. No doubt, he's watching porn with his hand down his pants."

Frankie shook his head in feigned gravity. "No, no, he wouldn't have the lights on if he was watching porn."

I raised my brow, leaning back inside the car. "And you know this because?"

"Ha ha ha. Stop worrying about your friends and go to bed and dream something normal for a change."

"Ha ha, yourself," I said. I shut the passenger door and watched Frankie back out of the driveway and head down Kingston Road, toward his other friends I had no connection to.

A rustling of sharp green leaves pulled my attention toward the yellow glow emitting from Mr. Coleman's basement. I shuddered and then inhaled sharply, telling myself that maybe, like Avo and Dad said, he really was just a lonely old guy passing the time down there in that basement tinkering, reading, or obsessively doing laundry like old people might do when they're alone. Maybe he even chose to be alone, like me, having no one to be in a relationship with.

I scuffed the gravel under my feet. *Unlike Gwen*, I thought, *even if the guy she chose to be in a relationship with didn't seem like he deserved her.*

The basement went dark, leaving me to wonder if we'd ever find out the real story—if there even was one, about what went on in Mr. Coleman's house. As the rest of Mr. Coleman's house remained dark, I also wondered whether or not Gwen might come to her senses about Andrew.

Under the dark night sky, my feet suddenly felt stuck in place, as if I couldn't physically move. A chill coiled through my body like a snake, followed by a grayish-white image forming in my mind. Thoughts began forming of ice on a pond during the winter—the dangerous kind, with the potential to crack.

Then it left, as quickly as it had arrived, though the message stayed with me. The problem was, I didn't know who the information pertained to.

CHAPTER THREE

My father didn't say much during the drive to the station the following Thursday night. I bounced my leg against the gray leather seat, my small frame always making me feel swallowed up in Dad's F-150 like Goldilocks in the too-big chair. I alternated between staring out the window as we drove past the extended brick library in the center of town and counting each silver minute on the dashboard clock. I needed to be early for this second class.

Dad kept twitching his shoulder, a habit he displayed whenever he felt stressed. It made me realize how little my father really knew about me or my life. I bit the side of my thumbnail, honing in on a hangnail as I took in St. Bridget's church with the slender white cross atop the steeple. We didn't go to church much anymore, except for holidays when Avo made my father and me go so we could show the good people of Hanley how we had carried on without my mother just fine. I yanked out the hangnail with my teeth.

A call came in on Dad's cell phone from the shop, which of course he accepted. When had he ever hit decline? I scrolled through my phone, secretly wishing I had the kind of father I could talk to about my feelings about the workshop, and about Gwen. Things felt different now that she was engrossed in her crazy Andrew obsession, to the point of keeping me preoccupied all week, unable to focus on the exercises Allison had given us for homework.

Viewing post after post of kids in school having fun doing things I couldn't care less about, I experienced a stabbing pain in my throat. I couldn't talk to Dad about Gwen, the workshop, or any of those kinds of things. He never even asked how the first night of class had gone or apologized for being unavailable to drive me. He probably still hoped the remote viewing workshop was some phase I might be going through, you know, wanting to learn more about exploring dreams, intuition, and psychic phenomena—like teenagers who vape, smoke pot, or get into witchcraft as a way of rebelling against their parents—and that I'd quit or something halfway through.

My father's only focus this past week, regarding me, anyway, was the "dumbass idea" of riding a bike for five miles on the main road in a state of panic, which could have gotten me killed. He never mentioned the fact that his being unavailable to give me a ride was what contributed to the chaos.

"Are you sure you want to keep doing this thing?" he asked, swiping at the end of his nose after he finished his call. The tone in his voice told me someone at the shop had done something that pissed him off.

"Yeah, Dad, I committed to taking it for the whole four weeks," I said under my breath. Sections of stained glass atop the small hill where the Lutheran church perched shone through the shadowy hedges.

"With all due respect to Len, I don't think taking some four-week course is gonna change your life. Don't get me wrong or anything, Len's been a good friend to our family, but I don't think it's gonna do what you think it's gonna do. I mean, hey, if it's what you want, that's great. I just think you could be working, going out, doing other things with kids your own age," Dad said. A Carrie Underwood song played on the radio, the only country music my father tolerated, probably because she was pretty.

"That doesn't sound very supportive," I said. Watching the sun begin to set in my side mirror, I caught sight of my furrowed brow, reminding me how intense I could be.

"I'm driving you, aren't I?" Dad said, his tone gruff, reminding me of that time those people from the Jesus Christ Church of Latter Day Saints showed up at our house, and he slammed the door in their faces. Without him seeing, I half-heartedly waved out the window from the living room couch, hoping they wouldn't be mad at me.

Under the glove compartment, I flicked my ankle back and forth and fidgeted with my necklace—the 14-kt. gold dragonfly Gram had given to me a year before she died, when I turned thirteen. Dragonflies were the spiritual sign representing my mother. I felt the grooves in its wings, rubbing my fingers back and forth across the muted gold.

"Look, if you're gonna get anxiety, I don't think continuing this thing is a good idea. I wouldn't think you would, either." Dad uttered that last part under his breath. I knew he was referring to how he had taken me to the hospital last year for a mental evaluation in the wee hours of the morning after I sensed my mother in my bedroom. As if what had happened to her—having hallucinations as a result of taking drugs and drinking too much—might also happen to me.

"I'm not anxious, I'm nervous," I said. We drove past a guy washing an old Pontiac Sunbird convertible in a driveway while his dog barked on a leash.

I hadn't told my dad that I never even took one of those stupid green pills he wanted me to take. I didn't plan on ever going down that path. Especially after I read something online about the potential side effects of anti-anxiety and sleep medications, which sealed the deal at *numbing of the mind.*

I wanted to learn more about my dreams and why they came to me, not stop them in their tracks.

"Anxious. Nervous. That's the same thing in my book," Dad said. He changed the channel after the Carrie Underwood song ended. Classic.

"Nope. Anxious sounds clinical. Nervous sounds normal," I said, staring straight ahead at the cars driving in front of Dad's truck on Route 139. "Cops and detectives are taking the class. They're normal."

My father's eyes narrowed as he took his foot off the gas pedal. A thought entered my mind from that faraway place that maybe Dad wanted me to be late. "Normal like wanna-be-detective Bobby Dempsey?"

I pinched the bottom of my thigh. "Why not? He seems normal."

Dad looked over at me. "From what you know of him . . . which better not be much."

I sighed. "There are also other people, including women, taking the class."

"Cops have to take those classes if they wanna move up the ranks," Dad said, switching on his blinker. "This isn't your job, Devon. You have a job when you graduate, working for *me*. Unless you're planning on becoming a detective now?"

My cheeks turned pink, highlighting my mom's Irish genes atop my otherwise olive Portuguese skin. How did my father know that some of the detectives weren't genuinely interested in developing their intuition, the same way I was? Could he even consider a perspective other than his own?

He seriously thinks he controls my world.

I pinched the bottom of my thigh a second time, hard, feeling the bruising in my skin, which weirdly made me feel powerful. I knew my father expected his business to stay in the family, but I didn't want the future my father had planned for me—working the front desk and doing administrative work at Alante's, the family auto-body business my grandfather had established years ago. It was where my father and Uncle Rob had both worked after high school, and where Avo did the books once a month to keep the money in safe hands. I loved my family, but I didn't want that future.

Closing my eyes, I took a deep breath as Dad drove into the station at a slow crawl. Even though he knew my dreams and visions had proven to be true, and that Detective Len was the one who encouraged me to take this class in the first place, my father still didn't, no, *wouldn't*, support a future—even a part-time one—involving something other than what he wanted for me. That made for two important people in my life—my best friend and my father—who had let me down in the last seven days.

"You're on time tonight, young lady," Len said as I jumped out of the truck before Dad even stopped at the curb. Len held open the heavy glass door with one of his chubby hands, his other hand clutching a black, three-ring binder against his leg. "Bobby'll get you signed in in the conference room."

"Yeah, sorry about that," Dad said, shaking hands with Len outside the truck. "She forgot to remind me last week and, you know how it is, I worked late at the shop."

I shot Dad a look before stepping inside the glass doors. *Seriously? You're apologizing to Len to make yourself look good, but not to your own daughter?*

"I'll be here at 9:30," Dad called after me, which had far less to do with him being a timely parent and way more about making sure I wasn't spending any more time with Bobby Dempsey than he deemed necessary.

CHAPTER FOUR

As everyone settled in their chairs, Allison sipped coffee from her black and silver thermos without making a sound and drew a black bell curve on the whiteboard. The area on the left she labeled, *Don't Get It,* underneath the bell of the curve, *Decent Ability,* and on the far right where the curve leveled off, *Innate Ability/Gifted.*

"Some of us are naturally gifted with multisensory perception," she began, red dry-erase marker in hand. "Others develop the skill, usually from interest, like anything else, since you tend to learn better when something holds your attention. Some people develop the skill after being exposed to trauma and some women are actually known to develop the skill while pregnant, both theories becoming popular in the current research.

Therefore, most of you are here to learn the remote viewing techniques offered in this introductory class to develop your intuition through discipline, to complement the work you are doing, with your left-brain, in the field. Some of you, though—who will be revealed over these remaining three weeks—may already innately possess the skills needed to speak the language of intuition and to potentially help the department solve cases."

I pulled my chair closer to the table, careful not to hit Bobby's leg. If I killed it in this class, well, then maybe, I could someday do this for work. Hank's watch ticked at the end of the table. If I could use the information that came to me in my dreams in order to help detectives solve real cases, even on a part-time basis, that might make working for my father easier to manage.

My body buzzed at the idea. *Part-time work, using my skills, as a detective.* I watched while Allison took another graceful sip from her thermos. *Screw math and science and every other stupid class I can't stand. Not that I can't do the work in my classes. I can. I just don't see why someone like me needs to learn things that I don't ever want to use in my life. I don't even remember what I've learned one year to the next. Now I don't care so much.*

Allison continued, tapping the marker against the board, "Therefore, if you don't have good intuition, or aren't interested in the subject of multisensory knowing from a distance, you likely wouldn't be here. Unless of course, you're simply fulfilling a class requirement."

Walter snickered and glanced back at Ed, both of whom had their beefy arms snug against their chests.

Negative thoughts started to creep their way into my excited brain. *Damn. Maybe Dad's theory was right. A couple of officers likely did take the class just to keep their jobs.*

I stared back at the whiteboard, at the classifications of people with regard to intuition. My father definitely fell on the left side of the curve, in the group of the *Don't Get It.* I realized nearly everyone I knew actually existed in this category. Except maybe for Gram—who passed away the summer before I entered eighth grade—who sort of spoke this language.

Gram believed in paying attention to the signs from Spirit—birds showing up at just the right time, finding heart rocks, chills running down your spine during certain moments, stuff like that—things she learned from taking a couple of angel-type classes in her later years. After my mom died, she said, she had become "more open to those kinds of things."

With my ankles crossed under my seat, Bobby leaned his broad chest across the table—a light blue color instantly swirling inside my mind—and asked Hank for one of the yellow number-two pencils that lay in abundance on the side table next to the coffee and snacks.

I let the light blue color settle around me like a soothing mist of rain. The scent of clean-smelling aftershave lingered as Bobby sat back in his seat. I felt myself fall into that welcome trance that happened whenever the information from that faraway place showed up.

Unpretentious. Caretaker. Friend. Protector.

The words arrived like fragrant bath bubbles floating in the air.

I gripped my thumb with my right hand to pull me out of the thoughts and sat up straight in my chair. With one strike already against me, I couldn't afford to space out the way I did in school.

Just then, the door flew open. A sixty-something, busty Middle Eastern woman blazed into the room. I felt a pull, a strong sensation like a magnet, trying to yank me from my chair. Instinctively, I gripped the sides of my seat.

"Sorry, dear, sorry everyone," the lady apologized, with a commanding, throaty voice. I imagined that same voice laughing along with her family around a large kitchen island filled with exotic dishes during the holidays.

She excused herself for being absent last week while she unbuttoned a lightweight cape fastened at her throat. Then she plopped herself down in the seat behind me like a sack of potatoes and fished into one of her bags for a notebook and pen.

Maybe things were looking up, I considered, as Walter glanced over at another guy in the front row with a barely concealed look of horror on his face. Apparently, I wasn't the only one in the class who now stuck out for less-than-professional behavior.

I peeked back over my shoulder, the way Avo always told me not to do in church. I decided the self-assured woman didn't look like either a cop or a detective. She looked more like a modern— though shorter and plumper—well-to-do wizard.

Allison smiled at the woman as if she hadn't been interrupted—a bit nicer than the way she had barely smiled at me last week, which probably had to do with the whole millennial factor. She proceeded to scrawl across the whiteboard: *Remote Viewing.*

"Tonight we'll be learning how to access information from the realm we cannot see," Allison said. Her enunciation clear and crisp, reminding me of how snow crunches under your feet during the first snowfall.

Sitting close to the edge of my chair, information floated into my mind about how hard Allison worked, how serious she took her job, something about her work being the most important thing in her life. A detective named Brendan in the first row whistled an out-there sci-fi tune about the "other realm" comment, and I took the opportunity, as much as the information interested me, to refocus.

Pursing her neutrally painted lips into a patronizing smile as if she had heard this sort of remark a zillion times, Allison commented, "That's right, you'll be learning how to move from a typical five senses point of view—taste, sight, smell, hear, and touch—to a multisensory point of view, with the purpose of obtaining data for your work. Scientists, artists, mediums, detectives, and stay-at-home moms all hold the same capability to tap into that unfamiliar realm of communication, regardless of education, job title, credentialed training, or age."

Though Allison didn't look in my direction, I wondered if she added the age comment for my benefit, which, along with the thoughts that had come into my head about her apparently less-than-stellar personal life, made me warm to her a little bit more.

For the next hour and a half, with my hands folded under my chin, I became captivated as Allison referenced Max Planck, the father of quantum physics, and Albert Einstein and the optical delusion of consciousness. This caused me to think about the stereotypical, crazy-haired Einstein referenced in physics class that I never paid attention to before, in a different way.

But as soon as I started getting excited about learning about something far more interesting than geometry or the fact that my leg was just a few inches from Bobby's underneath the conference table—something I would have normally wanted to share with Gwen as soon as class ended—thoughts about Andrew kept firing into my brain like annoying mosquitos attacking me on humid summer nights, even after you use bug spray.

"Connection?" Bobby asked ten minutes later during the break. He sat back and lifted the front of his chair off the floor, which made me feel comfortable for some odd reason, almost like I could picture him in one of my classes at school.

"What do you mean?" I asked. The rest of the class helped themselves to the coffee and small packages of peanut butter crackers and pretzels located on the side table.

"You're writing a lot," Bobby said. He jerked his chin toward the three-quarter covered lined pad of paper.

"It's so interesting," I said, wondering if I sounded like an absolute geek.

I took a sip from the eight-ounce Poland Spring bottle Hank had placed with a grunt in front of me, my drinking less about thirst and more about giving me something to do with my hands.

"That's good," Bobby nodded. The way he said *good*, not like mocking me, but almost happy for me, was mature, different from kids in my classes who might make fun of you for liking a subject so much.

My shoulders relaxed. I glanced down at myself, grateful I looked a lot better this week in a plain navy top and denim skirt—

without Gwen's help—and my hair in a neat, low ponytail. We sat quietly for a second until an officer named Paula, clutching a manila folder in her hands, started talking to Bobby about something she needed from him, some administrative stuff regarding a confidential case.

I grabbed my phone from under my chair, acting like I had important things to do too, when the wizard lady behind me, who had made the grand entrance, tapped me on my shoulder.

"You must be the budding forensic psychic Len told me about," the woman said, sitting back and crossing her stout legs. She munched on a pretzel from a small serving-size bag.

I turned fully around in my chair.

Forensic psychic.

Was that what I was? Or wanted to be?

I noticed the ruby-red ring on the woman's right hand, wondering what the kids at school would think of me being called a forensic psychic, since I had only ever been called a snob—or aloof. I didn't talk to anyone, really, outside of Frankie and Gwen.

"I'm not a fan of the word psychic, either," the woman said with a grimace, as if she could read my mind. "I prefer medium. Well, for what I do, anyway. The name's Gloria. I've been doing this work for twenty years, though only with Len and his team in recent months—part of a referral. I live up on the North Shore. Len asked me to sit in on the class. Got to earn your treads for each department, even if you already know how the work is done. You'll learn that if you want to do this work in the future, my dear."

A medium? Like someone who communicates with people who've passed?

Allison flicked the lights off and on, requesting everyone to take their seats. "Nice to meet you," I said, again feeling that magnet pull. "I'm Devon."

"Okay, next we'll be practicing a basic remote viewing exercise," Allison said, pressing a few keys on her laptop to follow her notes. *Allison's father taught her to be thorough; he was a professor of some sort, in the sciences.* "The exercise is simply to flex your intuitive muscles before we work on an actual, previously solved case approved for educational purposes. But that's next week. For now, get yourselves comfortable. You're going to learn to clear your minds."

I set both feet on the carpet in my first-ever attempt to be the best student I could be. I listened as Allison instructed us, in a clear, quiet voice, to take a few deep breaths. She turned down the lights, asked us to close our eyes, and guided us in a brief meditation. A recording of running water played in the background, mostly drowning out the voices of other officers passing by the closed door in conversation.

A few minutes later, as I tried to keep all the nagging thoughts I had in my head at bay and the voices of the people in the hall out of my mind, Allison told us to now immediately focus on minds on our "target," an inanimate object she had hidden somewhere in the building.

"With your eyes remaining closed," Allison said, using a louder and more commanding voice as she strolled across the rug at the front of the darkened room, "identify the material this object is made of. Is it shiny? Dull? Rough? Soft? Take a moment to consider what you sense, what you might see in the space behind your eyes."

Immediately, my entire body began to vibrate to the point where if someone's eyes had been open, they might have been able to see it. It felt like someone had plugged my finger into a socket. Something was happening. I knew this was my chance.

Except, Andrew's face suddenly appeared in my mind, with that annoying cocky grin Frankie and I couldn't stand. An urge pulsed through my veins, a feeling of wanting to push Andrew out of my way. The urge took me by surprise, anger usually more Dad's thing than mine.

I shifted in my seat, trying to shake off the unwanted images clouding my brain. I couldn't focus on anything besides Gwen and Andrew and the fact that she made him her priority.

"Identify whether the object is large or if you can hold in your hand," Allison continued.

I stared at the blank slate in my mind, like an old school blackboard. Only fuzzy dots appeared in the distance. Dots so meshed together, I didn't know if they were really even dots, like how static appears on TV after being interrupted by satellite.

A guy in the second row cleared his throat. Did he have trouble identifying the target too? I slid my foot under my chair. Would Bobby identify the target before I did? What if I didn't identify the target at all?

I bounced my leg against the seat, praying panic wouldn't overtake me.

"Now, I want you to decide what the object is used for," Allison said. "Let the purpose of the object speak to you. Trust in the multisensory language you are learning."

Fuzz appeared once again on my mental screen. This time like dust dancing in the sunlight, as if the dust was deliberately playing with me, taking pleasure in making me feel like an epic fail.

My heart pounded hard in my chest, panic rising fast inside my body. If nothing came to me, would Len think he made a mistake by allowing me to participate? Would Allison report to him that I didn't do well for the second week in a row?

An ink-like feeling spilled out from my heart, filling the rest of my body with a feeling of dread, of inevitable failure.

"Take another minute to consider the object's location," Allison said. "When you're ready, open your eyes, and begin writing down what you received."

I didn't need another minute. I needed another hour. To see beyond the static. The nothingness. I bit hard on the side of my thumb, desperately seeking another hangnail.

Bobby jotted something on his paper, covering the yellow-and-blue-lined sheet with his hand, the way smart students do in school when other kids try to cheat. He looked over at me with a playful side smile, which, on a different and better day, would have made my stomach jump.

Allison turned on the overhead lights, asking, "What brave soul wants to volunteer?" The lines around Allison's eyes made her look tired from lack of sleep. And stress. *Definitely stress.* I could feel the thoughts barreling their way toward me about her personal life.

I clenched my jaw in annoyance, ceasing the connection like ripping a cord out of a wall. I didn't need information on

Allison, I needed it on the stupid object sitting somewhere in the police station.

A thirty-something-year-old officer named Chris, the lines of his tank top visible through his light blue uniform shirt, raised his left hand in the front row. "I have no idea how to do this, or how to quiet my mind, but I'll give it a go. What came to me was a small gray box, like a pencil case, to house pencils I guess. Fascinating, I know."

The class laughed in unison while Walter, the detective who had tried to intimidate me last week, slapped Chris on the back. "That's because you're such a fascinating guy," Walter said nice and loud, causing Chris's pale cheeks to go red.

Allison, however, had no emotion on her face to indicate whether Chris was right or wrong or whether Walter was simply an asshat—which I could validate he was, because Dad had talked about him once when Walter didn't pay a bill on time for service on his wife's used Volvo. Allison simply wrote the words "gray/small/pencil case" on the board. "Thank you Chris. Next?"

"The object's color is silver," Gloria said. "I sensed a knife. Used as a tool or a weapon."

Allison wrote "silver/knife/tool/weapon" on the board while a broad-shouldered female officer named Lisa made some horror-movie reference to the officer seated next to her. "Excellent. Who's next?"

The rest of the class remained quiet, silently comparing their answers to the contrasting adjectives and nouns written on the board. Either no one wanted to look like a fool or to risk catching crap from Walter. I glanced down at my blank sheet of yellow paper, and then reached down and itched my ankle, the way I did in high school when I didn't want my name called.

"I'll try," a younger female officer with strawberry-blond freckles named Lynette said with her hand raised. I wondered if Lynette and Bobby were friends, since they seemed closest in age compared to the others in the group. "I saw a gray garage. Like an auto mechanic garage. The purpose? No clue. Seemed more like a place than an object to me. It doesn't match what's on the board though."

Allison wrote Lynette's key words on the board. "Which means nothing. Remember, don't rely on your left brain for remote viewing purposes. Anyone else?"

Behind me, Gloria rifled through one of her bags, making me think that maybe she was bored.

"I saw two circles, a pair of reading glasses, I think, no real color. I'd say steel around the rims," Ed said, dropping his pencil on the pad of paper and rubbing his forehead. "I didn't really get it."

The dry-eraser marker squeaked as Allison wrote Ed's descriptions across the board. Then she turned back to the class with a pleased look upon her face. "All right, let's stop here. I'll have someone head down to the lobby and return with the actual object." She pointed to Pete, a cop with a beer belly at the end of the first row.

In the few minutes Pete took to return, Allison explained to the rest of us the importance of letting our preoccupation with the outcome go and to try to resist the urge to analyze the information we received. She told us instead to surrender to and trust whatever data comes.

I scuffed the floor with my sandals, wondering if Allison was just trying to make those of us who didn't contribute, or get anything at all, feel better, in her no-nonsense, all-business, probably-already-did-this-and-got-an-A kind of way.

A minute later, Pete sauntered back into the room. He held a sealed manilla envelope out straight with his chapped hands, like he was handing off a baby in need of a bath.

"Well, we know there ain't no garage in there," Walter said, elbowing Lynette.

"Hold that thought," Allison said, unfastening the envelope.

A few seconds later, we all watched in silence as Allison retrieved a small, silver wrench from inside the padded package.

"Silver," Allison confirmed, holding the wrench in the air. "Also, could be seen as gray. And," she said, pointing to the phrase on the board, "it's hand-held. It's also considered a tool, and an object that is most certainly found in an auto mechanic's garage."

Walter turned with a not-so-bad-kid look on his face and then high-fived Lynette.

"Therefore, most of your data had pertinence and touched upon valid elements of the wrench, which in this case, was used as a weapon," Allison said. She placed the wrench on the table and picked up her thermos to take a sip. "On that note, I'll see you all next week."

Everyone stared at the board in contemplation for a minute before standing to leave. Bobby and I remained seated.

"So, what'd you get?" Bobby asked. He stretched out his long arms, cracked his back.

"You tell me first," I said, lifting my chin, trying to appear confident, hoping he had nothing on his paper that matched the board either. That way we could both commiserate together.

Bobby laughed and slid his information in front of me.

Metal, he scratched in pencil, in handwriting that was neither messy nor neat, *like a laptop. Square. Hand-held. Provides info?*

I felt like someone let the air out of my balloon. "Wow, good for you," I said, trying not to let my voice sound defeated.

"Now you show me."

With a painful lump in my throat, I pushed the yellow pad toward him, exposing my blank sheet of paper.

He gently elbowed my right arm. "Don't be frustrated."

I shrugged my shoulders, as if I didn't care, as if this class didn't matter at all to me, when all I really wanted to do was disappear, and maybe die. "You weren't so far off," I managed to say, "you must be psyched."

"I got the metal, right?" he said, with a self-deprecating laugh, which I wasn't sure was for my benefit, so I wouldn't feel worse, or if Bobby was just a naturally humble, awesome kind of person. His eyes crinkled when he smiled. I wished I didn't like it so much.

"Right," I said. I felt that anxious feeling in my stomach pick up speed. I prayed to Gram that I wouldn't have a panic attack right then and there. Cause if I couldn't do this basic exercise, how was I going to do the bigger stuff I wanted to do? I wanted to help people who might be in danger and do something about it before anything bad happened, unlike what I let happen with Denise last year, when I didn't trust the information. Did I even have a chance to prove myself now with only two classes left?

I could hear Frankie in my head chanting, *Wait, what's this? Zero for two, my friend! Better luck next time Miss Sad and Sorry!* and all of the other annoying stuff he said whenever we used to play Madden NFL or video games of any kind, even supposedly in the manner of fun.

"C'mon, that was only the first exercise," Bobby said as he rose and then pushed in his chair like someone who had learned good manners from his mother. "The department has you here for a reason. Next time you'll hit a home run."

"Thanks," I said. I pushed a strand of hair out of my face that had fallen from my ponytail. I wanted to say more. I wanted to tell Bobby that I was determined to do well, that I had to be here for a reason, that I couldn't imagine the dreams, the intuition, the sleepless nights not having a major reason in my life. I wanted to tell him that I felt I was supposed to help people.

But I couldn't find the words.

My head spun as I left the station a few minutes later with thoughts of Gwen, of Andrew, of failure, bombarding my mind. If their stupid drama kept occupying my thoughts, which was likely since it didn't sound, *or feel*, like Gwen and Andrew were breaking up any time soon, how would I focus next week in order to have some basic kind of success?

CHAPTER FIVE

Around three-thirty in the morning, a scraping sound, caused by one of Mr. Coleman's old, overgrown, low-hanging pine tree branches scratched the shingles on the side of our house, rousing me from sleep. A succession of dreams continued to ripple under my eyelids.

I kept my eyes glued shut, attempting to stay in that lucid state, a state I preferred over my waking one. I recalled the first dream. The little, frail, blond girl—the one who frequently appeared to me in my dreams—sat alone again, with her knees curled to her chest, in that cold, dank basement.

This time, though, I could see the frills on the hem of her sleeves.

"Who are you?" I whispered in the dark of my own room.

Was the five- or six-year-old girl, with the hollow eyes like she was a ghost of herself, simply serving as a lighter-haired version of me? I had always believed that's what the recurring dream meant—a metaphor of sorts for my life, since the girl seemed to be the same age I was when I ended up left alone without a mother.

Lying still against my sheets, not wanting to move a muscle for fear of the dream extinguishing like a flame on a blown-out candle, I waited for an answer. As if, for once, one might come to me upon my instantaneous request.

Nothing.

My body grew heavier, sleepier, in the waiting, in the wanting to return to the dream. I imagined being able to slip into the dream space and sit beside the little girl in order to find out more information. As much as she freaked me out whenever she showed up in my dreams, another part of me felt comforted in this eerie way that was hard to explain. It was as though in the awful feelings of watching her sitting in that dark cellar alone, the experience made *me* feel closer to my mother, across some other space and time. I felt myself drift toward a light, a spinning tunnel of sorts, with no objection on my part. Just a letting go, a free fall, to where I didn't know.

With no warning, I got yanked out of the heavy feeling. As if someone gripped my ankles fast, and in one fell swoop, pulled me, mentally I guess, back into my bedroom.

My eyes shot fully open, the space around me black and dead silent.

There was another dream.

I stayed still, a slow sense of knowing something I maybe shouldn't. The knowing crept up my body like a spider.

Gwen. Something about Gwen.

I threw back the covers, grabbed my nearly filled dream journal out of the beside drawer, switched on the small table lamp, and then started scribbling down the details as fast as I could remember:

Andrew, who at first I thought was Dad, but then changed back to Andrew, was in a car, with a girl. A girl that wasn't Gwen. It was nighttime, somewhere like a party in the woods. The girl had blond hair, and a silver hoop belly ring, small but clear as day. Andrew had a sneaky look on his face—a character trait of a cheater, a liar. Just by looking at his face in the dream, I knew, without a doubt in my mind, that he was lying about something. But I also knew, without a doubt in my mind, that Gwen didn't know.

CHAPTER SIX

My forehead pounded during Environmental Science class the following morning. Since Gwen took mostly Honors and AP classes, and I mostly didn't, our paths hadn't crossed at school. This was good news, because I wanted to talk to Frankie face-to-face at lunch about the dream first. Before I planned on talking to Gwen.

I stared out the third-floor windows onto the empty, turf football field in an attempt to keep my eyes open. Mr. Campbell droned on and on about age population charts, something I would never have to know, or care to know, anything about during my lifetime. Even Bio, when we learned about genetic disorders and plants and stuff, was better than this.

My mind raced through the possibilities about the dream. I thought about how in the dream, Andrew started out as Dad, and then faded back to Andrew, like some sci-fi morphing of one person into another. It started to throw me off about my suspicions about Andrew—like maybe the dream was really about my dad cheating on my mother, like I heard he had, back in the day.

I cracked my knuckles under the table. How could you really know for sure? It wasn't like I could ask my father, or Andrew, in order to gain clarity.

"Devon, would you please give us the answer to homework number 32?" Mr. Campbell asked, peering slightly over his narrow eyeglasses.

"Huh?" I asked. My face turned magenta as I heard some of the students snicker. I didn't want anyone, especially Mr. Campbell, to think I wasn't trying or didn't do my homework. I did. I wanted to do well. I just couldn't focus.

"Michelle, how about you?" Mr. Campbell asked. He shook his head as he called on another girl, who apparently could focus with no problem, in the front of the room.

Wishing I was home, or anywhere else really, I wrapped my arms around myself and tried to act like I was listening so I wouldn't be judged. One thing I did know for sure in that moment was that learning these ridiculously specific subjects we were supposed to study in school—the ones beyond the basics of reading and writing and math that everyone needed to know so they wouldn't be clueless—might help somebody else in our junior class who had a future at college and stuff—but they weren't going to help me in *my* life. And they definitely wouldn't help me figure out the best way to tell Gwen about her cheating, lying boyfriend.

———————

"Someone's looking like they were up all night studying for Spanish, except that wouldn't be you," Frankie said, slapping his tray of food down on the cafeteria table. "What's the story, morning glory? Damn, I swore I'd never say that after my mother used to say that all the time and drove me nuts."

I moved as close to him as I could at the end of the large, crowded lunch table. "I had a bad dream last night."

"What else is new?" he asked, biting into his double chicken patty, part of his effort to put an extra ten pounds on his naturally lean frame.

"I need you to be serious right now. It was about Gwen." I glanced down the table to be sure Elsie and Breanna, two of the biggest gossip girls in the grade, weren't listening. "I need to know what you think I should do."

Frankie jerked his chin, acknowledging one of his cronies at the adjacent table, who straddled the long picnic-style bench seat with one of his tree-trunk-sized thighs. "Okay," he said. He stuffed a ketchup-laden French fry into his mouth. "What happened in your dream?"

I took a breath. "Andrew cheated on Gwen," I whispered. "Well, I don't know if it happened already, or it's going to happen in the future, but I saw him with someone else, some blond girl in a car, and now it's like I know something Gwen doesn't, which makes me feel like a bad friend. Do you know what I mean?"

Frankie shook his head, stuffed the napkin that he used to wipe his mouth in the empty carton of milk he just scarfed down on the lunch tray. "Man, this stuff doesn't let up for you, huh? Last year, you dream of some girl in town that gets attacked, *then she does*, and now Gwen gets two-timed? I'm feeling for you, my friend. Truly. Cause that information is *not* going to go over well."

I bit down on my lip, bounced my leg under the table. "I know. But you think I should tell her, right?" I didn't feel like sharing with Frankie at the moment how Gwen and Andrew's relationship messed with my success in the first two weeks of the remote viewing class and that if something didn't change soon, I might not have a chance at any career other than working for my father.

Frankie bit into one of the chocolate chip cookies that he unwrapped from the yellow and clear plastic package, half-listening to the guys at the table behind us who were laughing about something that happened at some party last weekend. "They're not my dreams, dude, they're yours. If you feel Gaston's up to something, I'll trust you on that. It's not out of the question. Girls look at him like he's a filet mignon—or maybe one of those veggie burgers all the girls order now since chicks are going vegetarian these days—anyway, Gaston knows it, even if he does seem pretty hooked on Gwen."

I pressed my sneakers into the floor, feeling for a second like I had become "that" friend, the one whose life always revolves around some other person's drama. "I have to tell her today. It's driving me crazy."

Frankie took a swig of his Pepsi. "Just know up front, D, she's probably going to take your head off. But hey, if you had a dream that some chick was two-timing me, even though that would never happen to a guy with my kind of swag, you better tell me so I can break up with her, as hot as she might be. At the very least, maybe if Gwen knows she can't trust him, you know, from one of your prophecies, she'll break up with him. Then he can strut back to Marshton, the town that doesn't officially have beach rights, where he belongs."

I bit on the pad of my thumb. "I'm going to tell her after tennis. Do you want to go with me?"

"Ha. No, thank you," Frankie said, after the fifth-period bell buzzed through the loudspeaker. He stood and gathered his notebooks and pencil with the worn-down eraser. "I don't want to be in that path of wrath. But being the kind of guy I am, you can call me for free therapy after your dream message has been delivered."

———

Later that afternoon, I sat at the kitchen table staring blankly at my Forensic Remote Viewing packet, waiting for time to pass. Pellets of rain rhythmically began hitting the back deck. Through the glass sliders, I watched the droplets of rain touch the gray floorboards, the ones Dad had been meaning to update for years with a fresh coat of paint.

As soon as the clock displayed 5:15, I yanked my hoodie over my head, simultaneously knocking to the floor the twenty bucks Dad had left me on the table to get something for supper. I left it there, pulled open the sliders, and stepped out onto the slippery deck.

Down the two splintered wooden stairs, past the half-empty bird feeder, I made my way across the wet grass, glancing up at my tree house in the back of our quarter-acre lot. As old as I felt, my tree house with the green-covered canopy still stood as the treasured hideaway that always made me feel the most safe and secure. And, if I'm being real, closest to Mom in heaven, which is supposedly what I said when I was five, after Gram bought it for me that summer after Mom died by suicide.

The rain hit the canvas canopy, streaks of water creating a contrast of lighter and darker green. Even now, I still loved the idea of climbing up and crawling inside its four wooden walls, especially whenever Frankie, Gwen, and I needed to hold one of our Mandatory Meetings, which is why I told my father he could never take it down, and that, no, I hadn't outgrown it, even though yes, I was seventeen.

I touched the wooden ladder at the base of the old oak tree as I grazed by, thinking maybe I should have asked Gwen to meet Frankie and me in the tree house for this conversation and how she'd take the news from my dream. She'd probably call Andrew and confront him right then and there, after she got over being mad and hurt, in order to have the upper hand.

Gwen was always fascinated by my dreams. Maybe she'd even break up with him on the spot.

I pushed back thorny brush along the path leading to Timber Lane. *Yeah, she'll end up confronting him, in her blunt, no-one-messes-with-me Gwen way.* She'd have to, to preserve her dignity. Gwen would never put up with that kind of boyfriend.

When I reached the bottom of the short path that connected our streets, I saw Gwen's mom's white Audi parked at the bottom of their driveway. Crossing the slick cul-de-sac in the pouring rain, I pulled my hoodie tighter around my head, thinking about how much of my childhood was spent at the Davidson's: making crafts for the holidays at the kitchen table, swimming in their in-ground pool while Frankie's mom and my dad worked in the summers, and sledding over and over again during snow days on their sloping lawn. When we were little that felt like whizzing down the side of a mountain. Those memories seemed so long ago—before my nightmares took hold of my life and brought me to being the unwanted bearer of bad news.

I reached the two brick steps in front of the Davidson's glass front door, the one that was always open so Beckett, their golden retriever, could view the comings and goings of the neighborhood. Inside, Kristina reached across their farm table, her dark brown hair pulled back at the nape, tidying the kitchen the way she always did to keep her home looking nice. I knocked and she turned in my direction.

"Come in from the rain, honey," Kristina said through the glass. She smiled as she opened the door, her eyes wrinkled on the sides in a way that looked so kind, I hoped she'd never get Botox. "What a nice surprise," she said, hugging me tight.

I could hear Dr. Phil's voice coming from the small television in the kitchen.

"I hope I'm not interrupting supper or anything," I said, bending down and scratching Beckett's neck.

"Don't be silly, honey. You're always welcome. Gwen just got home from tennis." Then, with a roll of her eyes, Kristina added, "Likely on her phone with you-know-who."

I pursed my lips in a fake smile, trying to appear neutral.

Then, in that voice she had that never sounded angry, Kristina called up the flight of carpeted stairs to Gwen.

"I'll be down in a minute!" Gwen called from her bedroom.

A hollow pit formed in the bottom of my stomach. Beckett's tail continued to wag, while the gold pendulum of the grandfather clock swayed back and forth in the corner of the front hallway.

"Come in the kitchen," Kristina gestured. "I need to make cookies for the team dinner in a couple of hours."

Guilty feelings spread to the corners of my body. I pushed the damp hoodie off the front of my hair in order to do something with my hands and followed Kristina into the kitchen.

"So, no second chances for Andrew's friend Jared," Kristina chuckled as she reached for a carton of eggs stored on the side of the refrigerator door.

"Definitely not," I said. I slid my sleeves farther up my arms, referring to the failed double date last year. Gwen's footsteps sounded across her bedroom upstairs.

"Don't you worry," Kristina said, daintily cracking two eggs into the bowl of the stainless steel mixer atop the tan and butter-colored swirled granite island. "You hold out for someone as special as you are."

I smiled and rested my knee against the side of the island where *Barefoot Contessa* cookbooks lined the three, low-lying shelves. On another day, I might have been up for talking more and maybe even making jokes about that epic failed date with Jared, since Kristina always appreciated my humor, but a pain seared inside my stomach. Pain accompanied by an image of a lightning bolt that flashed in my mind, reminding me of the message I needed to deliver to Gwen.

"Are you feeling all right, honey?" Kristina asked. She poured a cup of sugar in the mixing bowl.

"Just tired," I said. I bit my pinky finger, wondering if I should have just called Gwen on the phone.

Kristina dropped spoonfuls of batter on an empty cookie sheet. I recalled the psychic fair workshop she encouraged me to attend last year, in that motherly way she always had with me, when the dreams started interrupting my sleep. The workshop taught me that when the dreams didn't let me go, I needed to take action, no matter the other person's response.

"Hey, Dev," Gwen said as she entered the kitchen, her hair all wet and shiny after a shower. She looked like one of those exotic-island people, even though she was Italian and Jewish. "Everyone will love chocolate chip cookies, Mom. Sadly, I won't be having any, cause there's no way my boyfriend's going to have better abs than me on the beach this summer."

Kristina looked to the ceiling in exasperation as Gwen opened the fridge and grabbed a bottle of Dasani water. "Do you want to stay for the team dinner? We're getting pizzas from Mamma Mia's for the rest of the crew, and Caesar salad for me."

"No, thanks," I said, pushing my toe into the bottom of the island, as if that might slow down my rapidly increasing heart rate. "I came over to talk to you about something."

Kristina slid the tray of perfectly rounded cookies into the oven. "Don't mind me, girls, I have clothes that need folding." She set the Crate and Barrel timer and left the room, barely making a sound in her bare feet as she crossed the shiny hardwood floor.

"You good?" Gwen asked, before taking a sip of water. Her slender nose and dark hair resembled Kristina's, while her hazelgreen eyes and direct, all-business personality, which I felt might unleash at any moment when she heard about what Andrew did in my dream, resembled her father's.

I swallowed a wad of fear. "I had this dream last night, and . . . ."

Holding the Dasani bottle on one hand, Gwen leaned forward, wide-eyed. "Are you still not sleeping? God, I could never deal with that. What was it about this time?"

Nausea rose in my throat. "Actually, the dream was about you. Well, sort of."

Gwen took a large sip of water. "What do you mean?"

I lowered my voice. "Last night, I, okay, I saw Andrew hurt you."

The lines in Gwen's forehead creased. "What do you mean *hurt me*?" She looked over her shoulder toward the laundry room. The dryer suddenly started swirling. "Hurt me like the Denise case?"

I chewed on my lip, wishing Frankie had had the guts to be here. "No, not that way."

Gwen put her water bottle down on the counter. "Well, what way then? Just tell me."

Gwen's assertiveness was often like being hit with a blunt object. I blinked a few times, the deer-in-the-headlights thing. "Andrew cheated on you with some blond girl, okay? Well, I don't know if it already happened, or might at some future point, I couldn't tell the time frame or anything, I just saw him with somebody else, in a car."

Gwen closed her eyes and shook her wet head of hair like she was doing a double take. "Hold on, you wanted to let me know but you don't know for sure if it happened, or if it might? What kind of proof is that?"

My throat felt dry and scratchy, the way it did before I took exams. "It's not proof exactly, it's just the feeling I got. That he did or would. That he isn't as great as you think he is."

In the other room, a sneaker banged against the side of the dryer. "Why did you tell me that?" Gwen asked, her eyes narrowed.

I pressed the grooves of my dragonfly necklace against my collarbone, trying to keep to my mission. I knew Gwen might be mad and hurt, but she acted like I was the enemy, instead of her unfaithful boyfriend. "What do you mean?" I asked. "How could I not tell you that? I haven't stopped thinking about it since it happened in the middle of the night last night, not to mention the fact that I didn't sleep."

Gwen crossed her arms over her chest. "So, it's about you, then? Making yourself feel better by dumping that on me? I know you don't like Andrew after I told you he gets jealous of Frankie and stuff, but for your information, he's loyal. He's loyal *to me*. If anything, he's scared I'll cheat on him. That's why he doesn't like any guys talking to me. But you wouldn't understand."

I straightened my spine. "I never said I didn't like him. I don't like the way he made you upset the other night, but I never said—"

"Maybe your hidden feelings came out in your dreams or something," Gwen interrupted me. "Maybe you subconsciously want something bad to happen cause you don't like how he acts protective of me. Andrew gets jealous, but he wouldn't cheat on me. I know him."

Pictures of the Davidsons from happy years summering on Cape Cod adorned the black fridge behind Gwen. Could that have been what happened? Making something up without realizing it, because I secretly wanted their relationship to end? Just so it didn't interfere with my life? Did that even make sense?

A dark cloud formed in my mind, the kind of foggy scene that would block someone from seeing clearly when driving a car.

No.

My dreams didn't come to me out of nowhere—unless they wanted me to know something, to see that something wasn't right. That much I did know. I had learned that over the past year.

I looked up from the floor and stared directly into Gwen's eyes. "I'm sorry but that wasn't the feeling I got."

The rims of Gwen's ears turned red, that one nervous trait she had that was easy to hide to other people, but not Frankie and me. "Well, I can tell you my boyfriend of almost a year wouldn't cheat on me. Ever," she said. I noticed the bottle of water shaking slightly in her hands. "So thanks for that, and for coming over."

A tingling occurred in my chest. "What are you being so salty for? I'm not trying to hurt you. I'm trying to give you a heads up. I'd want you to do that for me."

The timer clicked, returning to its original position.

"Don't worry, Mom, I'll get the cookies," Gwen called to her mother in a snarky voice. "Just go home okay, so that my team dinner isn't totally wrecked. Oh, BTW, I hope this doesn't wreck *your* night, but here's a message for you that you might need to hear: this time your dreams are wrong."

I stood in place for a second, my thoughts fuzzy and confused. I wanted to snap my fingers and be home as I watched

Gwen take the cookies from the oven with a smug look on her face.

After a minute, when I finally felt like I could unglue my feet from the floor, I left the Davidson's house—past Kristina in the laundry room, past Beckett laying in the front hallway, past the crew of tennis girls being dropped off in the driveway. All without saying another word.

CHAPTER SEVEN

It was two-thirty in the morning when I abruptly woke to the sound of waves crashing on a beach. Not the calming, soothing kind when people lie in the sun on vacation or the kind you hear when you Google ocean wave sounds on your phone to relax. This was an angry torrent of waves that made me think of shipwrecks after a typhoon.

The little clock ticked on my night table.

I sat up and draped my legs over the side of my bed, trying to recall the other sounds, and the possible message, that had drifted away with my dream.

Seagulls.

Waves.

Nighttime sky.

Gwen.

Again.

Something about a party on a beach, I think. Would Andrew cheat on Gwen there? Was there anything else I could get?

Wait. Please don't go.

Like a balloon floating away, the fragments of my dream drifted along with it. I imagined desperately trying to grab the string.

I squinted in the darkness. Even though I couldn't recall much of the details, the message was the same as last time: My dreams weren't wrong. Something, or *someone,* was letting me know for certain that Andrew wasn't all he appeared to be—and that Gwen was blind to the truth.

CHAPTER EIGHT

"You two still aren't talking?" Frankie asked me the next night at Holly's.

"Nope," I replied. I vigorously scrubbed a stain next to the cash register to avoid having to look at Gwen, who waited on a customer with a fake, upbeat attitude at the take-out window.

"What's up, Gwen?" Frankie asked, like he was Switzerland, never wanting to get in the middle of things.

"Hey, Frankie," she said, her elbow brushing my back as she shimmied past me toward the middle freezer like I had cooties. I clenched my eyes tight. "I'll see you down the Strip tonight?" Gwen's voice overly sweet while she dug into the vat of vanilla.

"Absolutely," Frankie said. After Gwen headed back to her customer at the window, Frankie leaned closer to me over the counter. "Why don't you come with me down the beach? Maybe Gwen'll apologize to you after she has a few—that is, if you decide to get out and have some fun in your life for once. Besides, what else are you going to do? Stay home binge watching *Friends* for the hundredth time? Or read though your dream journals now that you're like a legit psychic at the police station?"

A jolt shot through my body, commanding my attention. I paused for a moment, weighing the idea of putting myself in a social situation that would most definitely make me want to crawl out of my skin, but yet put me smack in the middle of an environment where I could spy on Andrew. "Fine, I'm in, just don't leave me standing around by myself when your new football friends arrive."

I stashed the cleaner spray under the counter. I could fill Frankie in later on the real reason for my mission.

"Excellent choice. I sound like a waiter after you've selected a fine wine. And no one's got your back more than this guy," Frankie said, pointing toward his chest, while his cell phone pinged in his hand.

At closing time, Gwen and I hung our aprons on their hooks and signed out on the clipboard without a word. Outside, the taillights of Frankie's Jetta glowed red across the parking lot, music competing with his muffler as a rap song played through his open car windows.

I stepped outside where, parked a few feet in front of the door, Andrew immediately started his black Mustang, blinding me with his headlights. I swear it was on purpose.

"Hey, babe," Gwen said behind me, like she had been married for five years. She stepped daintily down the brick walkway in the fancy sandals she had just put on and leaned inside to kiss Andrew through the driver's side window, where he sat stony-faced with one forearm rested on the steering wheel.

"Hey," Andrew nodded in my direction as I scuffed past in my sneakers.

"Hey," I answered, trying not to act like I knew about the driveway drama at Gwen's house, plus the fact that he didn't like Frankie, or that I had two dreams about him being a cheater—dreams that messed with my sleep and my chance of career success, since it didn't seem like Gwen had told him any of these things. If she had, I wondered if Andrew would have tried to get her to stop talking to me too.

"See you down the Strip," Gwen called to Frankie, her big Vera Bradley tote slung over her shoulder. Frankie saluted with two fingers out his window. Standing outside Frankie's passenger-side door, I watched as Gwen made her way around the back of the car and then sunk down into Andrew's waxy-smooth passenger seat.

"Need to go home and freshen up first or anything?" Frankie asked. I chuckled while I moved a canister of muscle-building protein from the front seat into the back.

"I'm good," I answered.

I didn't care about looking pretty or having fun—my only reason for going to the stupid Strip was to keep an eye on Gwen's goon of a boyfriend.

———————

Fifteen minutes later, dozens of regular cars—Nissans, Hondas, Highlanders—along with a few luxury SUVs with private-school stickers on the back windshields, and one nice, shiny metallic red 1990 Mazda Miata convertible parked in the middle of two spaces, packed the nearly filled upper lot at Hanley's public beach. Frankie wedged his Jetta in front of a maroon Honda Pilot in the far corner of the sandy lot. No sign of Andrew's Mustang in sight.

"Here," Frankie said, reaching into his back seat and yanking a navy blue and gold Hanley football windbreaker out from a pile of McDonald's trash bags crumpled on the floor. "In case you get cold."

"You want me to wear something that was laying on top of trash?" I asked. "This could be a good reason why you're still single."

"Relax, the air will get at it." Frankie tucked cash into his socks and then stuffed his wallet into the middle console. The din of the high school crowd sounded from the shore, my social anxiety instantly causing me to scratch at my skin. "And what's up with Gaston not saying anything to me at Holly's? It's like he's annoyed that Gwen and I are friends or something."

"He probably doesn't like *anyone* talking to his girlfriend," I said, opting to keep the information Gwen shared with me private at the moment. "Even though, according to my dreams, *he* can do whatever he wants," I said. I got out of the car and scanned the parking lot while I yanked the French-fry-smelling sweatshirt over my head.

"Lame loser that he is," Frankie said, locking his car. I wanted to hug him for a second, the way he supported my dream information, the way Gwen hadn't.

"Meanwhile, the reason I'm here, no offense to you, is to keep an eye on the two of them. I had another dream last night."

"What happened now?" Frankie asked. He stashed the key in the side pocket of his hoodie.

"It was something about something happening on the beach, and the whole he's-not-the-boyfriend-Gwen-thinks-he-is kind of thing," I said, following Frankie, who trailed a big pack of kids toward the sea wall.

"I thought you said the first dream happened in the woods," Frankie said, right before heckling three of his teammates who lugged a cooler down the set of concrete stairs leading to the beach.

"It did." I looked around to see if Andrew's car had parked somewhere along the road. "But then I saw the beach in my dream last night, and I heard the waves. So I don't know if maybe things changed or what that means exactly, but when you asked me to go, there was no way I was going to pass up the chance to keep an eye on his potentially cheating self."

"Technically then, I'm like your accomplice spy," Frankie said, over his shoulder. "Do you want me to video him in the act if we catch him in any shenanigans? Though I don't know where he'd hide with the incoming high tide, my friend."

"Just keep an eye on him while you're with your friends," I said once we reached the top of the stairwell. "If you see anything funny, anything we can alert her to, then tell me, so we're both on it."

Orange sparks mixed with ash shot up from several bonfires lit along the shore where teenagers gathered in clusters the way they did in the hallways and cafeteria at school.

I cracked my knuckles. Since Gwen and I weren't speaking, I realized it was going to be harder than I thought to keep an eye on her with so many kids spread in zig-zag formations down the small parcel of public beach.

Counting the sixteen stairs leading down to the sand, I wondered how long this would go on, Gwen and I not speaking— the longest we had ever gone was in seventh grade, for only one day, when I told her, after she asked, that yeah, she had some fat around her belly since we ate ice cream basically every night during the summer.

"All right. I'll be your partner in crime. I'm just glad Gaston doesn't *live* in *our* town, so we don't have to see his arrogant ass at school every day. Meanwhile, my money's on you being next," Frankie said, zipping up his jacket once his feet hit the sand.

"Next for what?" I asked. I searched above people's heads, trying to spot Gwen in the crowd in case I missed seeing Andrew's car.

"A relationship. Dude, you're a catch," Frankie said, wrapping his arm around my shoulder. He nodded to some kid from school. "You just don't put yourself out there."

"I don't put myself out there because I have other things on my mind," I said, shoving him playfully in his side.

"With all those prophetic dreams you have, I don't blame you for not thinking about guys. Me? All I think about these days is shallow stuff," Frankie said, raising his voice above the country music coming from someone's speaker. "That's where we're different, my friend."

"You're not shallow," I said. I placed my hands on Frankie's shoulders, trying to keep the conversation going so he'd stay with me once he found his friends. "You're just going through a shallow phase."

Frankie glanced farther down the beach to find the football crew, the crowd he had gotten closer with sophomore year, when Janice, Frankie's mom, first allowed him to finally play football. "Keep in mind though, dude, it's Gwen's life. She's going to do what she wants to do without any direction from her BFFs from the hood. So you might as well have some fun while you're here. You never know—you might meet the guy of your dreams tonight—no pun intended."

A group of kids puffed on a joint and passed around a bottle of vodka a few feet away, beside the closest bonfire. "But there's such a fine selection to choose from," I said. "I wouldn't know where to start."

Frankie led me farther down the beach. "C'mon. Gwen will find you, especially if she's drinking, feeling the guilt and shit."

I followed Frankie in the grooves of his footsteps in the hard, dampened sand. It felt weird to me how he seemed to know everyone these days—a far cry from middle school, when the three of us hung out on the blacktop at recess, not caring what the more popular kids did.

I noticed a heavy-set kid from my English class, his face shadowy as he stood back from the crowd, with his nose buried in his phone as we trudged past. I wondered if he really cared about what he was looking at or if he used his cellphone to cover up feeling like he didn't fit in either and would rather be home watching TV on his couch.

Twenty minutes later, I stood off to the side of Frankie's new friend group and scrolled Instagram at the same time I kept looking around for Gwen. Between one post after another about someone's dumb made-up dance, I started to wonder whether she'd show up at all. Maybe they decided to go to Andrew's house instead. My heart felt like it shriveled inside my chest. I started to wish I went to bed early to catch up on sleep—until I heard my name being called.

Barefoot, Gwen stepped across the sand with one hand clutching her shoes and the other extended behind her with Andrew's hand in hers, as if they were one person now instead of two. *Gwandrew,* Frankie might say if he was standing next to me, instead of laughing at someone else's story as he stood next to a small bonfire with his muscle-head friends.

"Hey," she said, letting go of Andrew's hand after he stopped to talk to some guys from Marshton. I smelled the faint smell of beer on her breath. "I can't believe you're here." She looked over and then waved to Frankie, who opened his eyes wide at me, as if to say, *see?*

Gwen crossed her arms over Andrew's club Lacrosse team sweatshirt, her eyes glossy, the way she looked when she had the flu. "I thought about it on the way here. This is ridiculous, this whole us-not-talking thing. You hurt me and I said something that hurt you back. I'm sorry for that part. Let's just put it behind us. You know I believe in your dreams. It's just this time, well, I appreciate your worrying about me and everything, but I have a great boyfriend. Really. And I want you to be happy for me. Maybe we can agree to disagree about Andrew. Okay?"

The sand felt uneven under my feet. I shifted my stance, wondering if Gwen really felt sorry for what she said or if she only felt regret because she'd been drinking. "Okay," I said, after taking a minute to think about what else I wanted to say. The only thing I knew right then was that I had a better shot at watching Andrew if Gwen and I were in good graces.

Ten feet away, standing close to the fire, Andrew whispered and laughed with Jared, the teammate I dissed last year.

"Don't worry," Gwen said with a laugh, "I told Jared not to bother you. Even though now, of course, he considers you a total challenge."

"Awesome," I said, purposefully keeping my focus on Gwen.

"Anyway," Gwen said, "Just to let you know, Andrew apologized about the whole driveway incident—he said he just loves me so much, he wants to make sure no one else is in the picture."

No one else is in the picture I started to say, but Gwen turned away from me after Andrew called her over.

"Sorry," Gwen said, giving me a quick hug. "He made me promise I wouldn't leave him standing around since there's more kids here from Hanley. Glad we made up."

"No problem," I said. I watched Gwen strut back to Andrew like a puppy on a leash, while I stood alone, huddled inside Frankie's smelly sweatshirt, realizing I never got to speak. Andrew looked over at me with a smirk while he held Gwen tight around her waist. It made me question whether she *had* told him about my dream.

"I'll be right back," Frankie said in my ear. I noticed him look toward the seawall. A couple guys raised a large rectangular cooler over their heads, the crowd cheering them on like little minions.

Apparently only I considered this a stupid move, since the three of them stood visible from the parking lot, close to the open road, where cops constantly patrolled the area, looking for underage drinkers. A few minutes later, Frankie's scrawny frame was hoisted atop Zack Singleton's beefy shoulders. They began egging on another group of kids to have a beer-guzzling contest, making the two of them look like Davy and Goliath. I pinched a section of skin near my elbow, wondering if Dad acted this way when he was a football star at Hanley High.

Inky waves forcefully rolled onto the beach and then retreated, the heavy, whooshing sound causing me to shiver.

The sound, the darkness, calling to me, reminding me, of my dream last night.

An image of a rogue wave, the kind we learned about in eighth grade science class, rose up, high and haunting, inside my mind.

"What the hell?" I heard someone yell, their startled voice pulling me from my inner world.

Beside the roaring fire, I saw Paul Callahan, a senior at Hanley High, step back from a fast-approaching Andrew.

"Stop," Gwen said in a pleading tone, grabbing Andrew's arm.

"Were you staring at my girlfriend?" Andrew asked. His arms spread wide, ready for a fight—no, looking for a fight.

"What are you talking about?" Paul asked, the side of his face in a screwy expression.

"Don't deny it," Andrew said, moving toward Paul like an animal closing in on its prey.

"Chill out, kid," Paul said. He grimaced and turned to leave.

I watched as Andrew's beady eyes bore into Paul's back, right before he hauled off and sucker-punched him on the side of his face. He reminded me of Mike Tyson, the aggressive fighter my father liked to watch in the old boxing matches on TV. Mike Tyson if he fought in a one-sided boxing match, that is. "Don't tell me to chill out when you're looking at my girl."

I bit down so hard on my lip I tasted the blood. *What a scumbag.* He didn't even give Paul—a quiet, good kid who never bothered anybody as far as I knew—the respect or the opportunity to raise his hands to defend himself.

Paul held his hand over his nose that had started pouring blood. "You're a psycho," he said.

Some girl in frayed shorts ran to a cooler to get ice.

"Yeah? Look at my girlfriend again, and I'll get the other side of your face," Andrew said, pointing his finger while he spoke.

"Marshton punk," Paul mumbled under his breath, now clutching the dripping, paper-towel wrapped bundle of ice to his face.

"What did you say to me?" Andrew spat. He moved in again and then pounced on top of Paul like a black panther, punching him repeatedly in the face.

"Stop!" Gwen screamed. She tried to pull Andrew away to no avail. Then, Jared and some other Marshton kids jumped on Paul and added to the melee.

As if on cue, a fistful of Hanley guys added to the chaos, their arms and legs punching and kicking the Marshton thugs, while kids from both towns yelled and cheered.

I made a beeline toward the crowd to get Gwen out of the mix before she got hurt or someone got arrested.

"Dump the beer!" someone yelled from the parking lot. Police sirens wailed, rising in volume until the swirling, neon blue lights of three cruisers became visible to the rest of us standing down on the beach.

Sounds of beer cans clinked and clanked as they were tossed in the reeds lining the sea wall, kids emptying coolers fast. The fight began breaking up, people scattering in varying directions. I couldn't get to Gwen, who was in tears trying to calm Andrew down in the middle of the crowd, before I lost sight of her completely.

Four officers made their way down the cement stairs, flashlights in hand, interrogating kids carrying coolers and asking for identification, while two more stood at the top of the sea wall scanning the beach with searchlights, checking for underage drinkers.

I craned my neck searching for Gwen in the chaos before Jared pulled on my arm. "C'mon," he said, his breath reeking of alcohol as he pressed his other hand into my lower back. "We don't want to get busted."

I jerked my arm away hard. Jared muttered something under his foul breath. Noticing Frankie at the base of the sea wall, I pushed my way through a group of girls putting out half-smoked joints on their wet fingertips.

"What are you doing?" I asked. Frankie stuffed empty cans into the plastic green trash barrels in an attempt not to get caught. "Didn't you see that fight Andrew started? We have to find Gwen. I lost her."

Frankie pressed his car keys into my hand. "I hope he got his butt kicked. Right now, though, I'm helping my other friends not get busted. I'll meet you up in a few."

I sighed, ran my hand through the front of my unbrushed, ponytailed hair, and stomped toward the stairs. A group of Hanley kids in baseball caps stood at the bottom, witnessing two Marshton guys wearing soccer jackets—Andrew's cronies smack in the middle of the fight—being led up the stairwell in handcuffs by two of the officers.

Too bad you didn't get the guy who started the whole thing, I thought. A few feet away, Paul stood alongside a guy and a girl with ice pressed against his face, while he spoke to one of the officers.

Hoping to find Gwen in the parking lot, I followed a pack of kids up the stairs who were apparently leaving the beach for the next party. When I got to the top, a fourth officer made two girls in front of me dump beer cans stashed in their jacket pockets into a trash barrel. In the darkness, I noticed his face and crew cut felt familiar to me.

Bobby.

He glanced past the girls, in my direction, his brow furrowed. I couldn't tell if it was because of the task at hand or because he judged me, that I was here with all these other kids, doing this kind of thing, though he never asked me for identification.

I hope he doesn't think I drink. I shimmied past the girls, out of his stare and started scanning the parking lot for Andrew's car.

I dialed Gwen's number on my phone and then started walking the perimeter of the lot, ignoring the twenty or so teenagers gathered around one Hanley police cruiser where the two idiots sat in handcuffs in the back seat. When Paul and his friends drove out of the lot, I sighed, glad that he was okay enough to leave. Now I needed to know if Gwen was okay, after that ridiculous fight. I mean, everyone at Hanley High knew Paul Callahan had a crush on Gwen. He'd liked her ever since elementary school. She didn't like *him* though, so why did Andrew make such a big deal out of it? Maybe he was all messed up on pills or something, though he didn't seem the type.

Six rings. Gwen still didn't answer her phone.

I texted and then checked her Snapchat location, but it was turned off. Maybe someone else drove her home, and she didn't want Andrew to know. That'd be smart, in case he tried to follow her, which I wouldn't put past him, since he acted like a control freak. In ten minutes I planned to try Kristina, to be sure Gwen had made it safely home.

I checked the main road for Andrew's car, just in case. The only streetlight, on the access road a hundred yards away, it made it tough to see. I reluctantly turned on the flashlight app on my phone, not wanting to drain the battery. After tonight, Gwen would have to realize all the drama Andrew brought to their relationship. Then, maybe I wouldn't have to deal with my dream after all, since she'd dump Andrew before it had a chance to come true.

An actual flashlight ripped through the darkness, swaying between the cars still parked out on the main road. I turned, squinting in the glare.

"Sorry," Bobby said, lowering the flashlight. He snapped a piece of gum. I could smell the pink bubble gum, the kind I used to like when I was younger. "Everything okay?"

"Yeah, I'm fine," I said, tucking a strand of hair behind my ear. "I'm just trying to find my friend."

"I hope it's not one of the guys who just got busted for fighting, or the ones who had some stuff on them, cause you may have missed your ride."

"No," I said, standing on the other side of a green Toyota Corolla. "It's my best friend, Gwen, whose loser boyfriend started the whole fight down there and probably should have been one of the ones who got arrested, but it looks like you guys missed him."

"The kid whose nose was bleeding said something about that, but he didn't give us details." Bobby stepped agilely behind the Corolla. "What's the boyfriend's name and what does he look like, in case he's still around?" He started shining his flashlight between the other cars on the main road.

"Andrew Ferrara, but it's not looking good," I said. I hesitated giving Bobby all the information about Andrew that I knew. Reluctantly, I chose to honor the best friend code the same way I had with Frankie earlier—putting Gwen's feelings first before throwing her boyfriend under the bus. At least for now. "He probably made a mad dash out of here, cause he's slick like that. I'm just hoping Gwen got a different ride home. I'm waiting for her to call me now."

We re-entered the parking lot through the main entrance. I searched for Frankie's bushy head of hair in the rest of the crowd coming up from the beach. *C'mon, Frankie, we have to find Gwen.*

"Well, if the kid who got punched in the face pretty good decides to press charges, I'll know who to talk to. My partner and I can take you home, if you need a ride," Bobby said, clearing his throat. Standing like a tower with his six-foot, plank board frame, he waved one of the cars past. "What are you doing out here anyway? Some of these guys have got a bad reputation with the whole drug thing on the rise around town."

I raised one eyebrow. "What are you, my father? I already have one of those—and he's kind of like having three when it comes to my whereabouts."

Only when it came to dating, I reminded myself. Which made it less about me and more about him being in control of his only child.

Bobby laughed while he steered me out of the way of the next line of cars leaving the beach. "I kind of got that feeling the day you guys came into the station last year. Your dad would probably kill me if I didn't make sure you had a ride home, though, so I had to ask."

A chill ran through my body.

Whenever you get the goose bumps, Gram used to say, *pay attention to the signs.* Was I getting chills about Bobby or about Gwen? Where they good chills or bad?

Was Gwen okay? I chewed on my thumb.

"My ride will be up in a few minutes," I said, glancing at my phone to see if Gwen had texted as I headed in the direction of Frankie's car in the corner of the lot. "He's probably still down on the beach, you know, helping clean up or whatever." *Hopefully not in jeopardy of getting arrested while he gets rid of additional beer cans.* I may have hesitated about Andrew because of my friendship to Gwen, but I wasn't about to throw Frankie under the bus.

"Boyfriend?" Bobby asked, shining a light on Frankie's Jetta sitting unevenly parked in the corner of the lot. He never could parallel park, though he forbade me to razz him about it, since I still didn't have my license, even if that was my choice.

"Huh?" I asked, looking up from my phone.

Bobby jerked his head toward the beach. I tried not to stay stuck on the fact that he had the coolest mannerisms, smooth but not jerk-smooth, nice but not overly nice, I guess cool and nice at the same time is how I'd best describe it, even though I had nothing to compare it to, since I didn't know anybody else who behaved that way. Everybody I knew who even had some remote kind of swag was also a moron. "That guy trying to protect you or whatever he was trying to do while falling drunk over himself—is that your boyfriend?"

I bit my bottom lip, the thought immediately registering that Bobby had seen me before I had seen him. Bobby gestured to his partner near another cruiser that he'd be over in a minute. "No, that was some jerk from Marshton. Frankie's my ride, and he's just my friend. So, did Paul say he might press charges?"

Bobby stared at me for a moment, as if he was trying to see inside my brain. "He said he'd consider it when we gave him the option. Your friend's boyfriend sounds like a punk. We wouldn't want him going and doing this kind of thing again, especially if he was drinking or on something, or just whenever he felt like it, if he's that kind of guy."

"Whenever anyone looks sideways at his girlfriend," I mumbled under my breath, the night growing colder the later it got.

I pulled up Kristina's contact information on my phone. Had Gwen called her to be picked up? Kristina had a no-questions-asked policy if either Gwen or Livvy, Gwen's older sister, needed a ride home from a party.

I dialed Kristina's number. No answer.

"While you're waiting for your friend, what'd you think of the class?" Bobby asked. He shone the flashlight inside Frankie's car.

I cracked my knuckles after I caught my breath in my throat, which I probably would have paid more positive attention to had I not had Gwen's whereabouts on my mind.

"Well, since I didn't do that great the first couple times, I'm hoping for a better night this Thursday," I said, experiencing a sudden inability to take my eyes off the way Bobby's straight nose fit perfectly on his lightly tanned face.

"Len Dyer says he's expecting big things," he said, tucking the flashlight back into the pocket of his navy blue uniform. "I'm sure you'll impress us all. If you don't mind me asking, do you always dream the way you did about the Denise Franklin case or was that some sorta fluke thing?"

I felt my cheeks flush in the darkness. Kids talked and laughed, music playing in their cars as they drove past, leaving the beach. I hadn't really dreamt like that, *about crimes,* since the case last year.

"You don't have to answer if you don't want to," he said, his forehead wrinkled. Feelings stuck to me like Post-It notes; Bobby was empathetic, caring, concerned, trustworthy. Character traits revealed themselves to me, as if they were answers to questions I was asking without knowing I was asking, arriving from that other place, as if someone sent them to me, like receiving letters in the mail.

"No, it's okay," I said, standing there, phone in hand, under the night sky scattered with stars. I shuddered, hoping Bobby didn't notice. "I guess you could say it happens enough."

But I don't know *why*, I wanted to add.

A gust of wind kicked up sand across the cracked concrete lot.

"That must be tough," Bobby said. He shook his head, the way people do when they've heard something upsetting on the news but are simultaneously relieved it's not happening in their part of the world.

My stomach tightened. *Did he pity me? Or think I was weird?*

"Everything all right, officer?" Frankie asked behind me, his hands inside the deep pockets of his sweatpants, which I hoped at the moment didn't contain cans of beer.

Bobby turned, standing a few inches taller than Frankie. "Just waiting with Devon to be sure she's all set. You must be Frankie. You weren't part of the fight down there, were you?" Bobby eyed Frankie in a way that told me he was checking for signs of intoxication.

"Me? No sir, officer," Frankie said. He shook Bobby's outstretched hand. "Have you seen this frame? I'm not much of a fighter."

Bobby chuckled. "Anything you can tell me about the kid who might have started the whole thing?"

Frankie looked over at me. "Just that he's a blowhard from Marshton, but I'm sure my friend here may have filled you in on that, since I didn't see the whole thing go down. How do you know Dev, anyway?"

"Lots of wear and tear on those cruisers," Bobby said, referring to the fact that Alante's, my father's auto-body and towing business, serviced all the police cars in Hanley. I felt a warm feeling inside my chest that Bobby chose to keep the class between us, just in case I hadn't told Frankie. Or maybe it was just confidential information and he couldn't.

Frankie looked over at me first and then back to Bobby. "Right. Okay. Well, thank you Officer . . . ?"

"Dempsey. Drive safe," Bobby said, stepping back to allow Frankie access inside the car, while continuing to watch his movements. I felt grateful in that moment that Frankie never drank and drove.

"Always," Frankie said. He slid into the driver's seat and turned the key in the ignition while I got in on the passenger side. Opening the window, he added, "Good night, Officer Dempsey."

Once I buckled my seat belt, and he seemed satisfied that I was safe, Bobby put his palm up in my direction to say good-bye.

"Where have you been?" I asked as Frankie put the car in reverse. "Did Gwen text you? She's not answering her phone and neither is Kristina. I think we should go to her house to be sure she's there." I dialed Kristina's phone a second time.

"She didn't text me. She probably just had someone else drive her home so she could get out of here before the cops came, National Honor Society status and all of that," Frankie said. He turned his car around in the lot. "It still pisses me off, on a side note, that Calc kept me from achieving that milestone. Damn Mr. Corsica. Did you ever have him?"

"Frankie, focus!" I said, hitting him in the arm after I hung up the phone, Kristina not answering for a second time.

"I saw her with Andrew after the fight and then I lost her. Do you think she's all right?"

"Don't worry, dude, we'll find her. I'm more annoyed that Gaston made it out unscathed," Frankie said. He turned on the radio to the local hip-hop station as he drove behind two other cars leaving the beach. "On another note, it was kind of hard to take that cop seriously since he looks like he just graduated high school."

"Why?" I asked, glancing in my side mirror. "How old do you think he is?"

"I don't know, maybe twenty-two, twenty-three? Why? You interested?" Frankie said, turning to me with a surprised look on his face.

"Just wondering," I said. I sat on my hands. "Bobby's taking the same class as me, you know, at the station."

Frankie put on his blinker and turned out of the beach parking lot with one hand on the steering wheel. "Ahhh, boy was lying to me then about knowing you from Alante's."

I glanced sideways at Frankie. "I don't think he was *lying*. He just wasn't offering it up for conversation."

"As if you'd keep something from me," Frankie said, nudging my arm with his elbow. "Hey, maybe you guys'll work together on cases someday, like those detectives on TV."

I leaned my head back against the seat. "Let's not get dramatic. We have enough drama at the moment from Gwen. I don't know why she didn't just find me after the whole thing to come home with us after Andrew did Paul Callahan dirty."

Frankie shook his head. "Apparently they're hooked on each other."

"I'm going to text her again. It's been twenty minutes," I said, picking up my phone, moving my thumbs fast across the surface.

"Gwen's tough, D, she can handle herself. Remember when I posted that picture of the three of us and she didn't like it and came over and dumped a can of water over my head? I get that we were outside and that it was summertime, but still. Gwen doesn't put up with any baloney, as my grandpa used to say. Not from you, or me, or Gaston. Stop worrying. She'll be home safe and sound and, hopefully for your sake, single."

"Okay," I said. "Meanwhile, keep your eyes on the road. You heard Bobby. Drive safe."

Frankie turned to me, the wind whipping through the car as we headed down the access road. "You heard Bobby? Well, well, well. I think someone does have a crush on the baby-faced cop."

"So, you're admitting he's handsome then," I said, staring straight ahead. "By the way, thanks for staying with me, party boy. You and Gwen both MIA, I never could have predicted that."

The wind whipped through Frankie's hair as the car picked up speed. "I had to help my boys so they didn't get busted."

"Since when are your 'boys' more of a priority than taking your friend from the neighborhood home?"

My phone buzzed in my hand. "Finally!" I said, looking down to read the text.

"Hey, did you get out okay? We did! Thank God! I'm at A's house—it's all good! Just knew you were worried. Talk tomorrow!"

My heart sunk into my stomach.

Seriously? Hold on. *She didn't even acknowledge the fight.*

"She with Andrew?" Frankie asked as I sat in silence.

"Yup," I said. I shut off my phone and stuffed it under my leg. "Just take me home."

CHAPTER NINE

The following morning, the teakettle whistled. With my eyes at half-mast, I made myself a cup of chamomile tea in an attempt to relax after yet another sleepless night. I poured the hot water into my World's Favorite Daughter mug, the one perched right next to the World's Favorite Dad mug. The quiet of the house, along with the Dunkin' Donuts bag containing one blueberry muffin on the counter, reminded me that Dad wouldn't be home to cook Sunday breakfast.

I grabbed the container of honey from the cabinet next to the sink—the container that sat perched next to the orange bottle of Vitamin D that Dad now took faithfully every morning ever since he started dating Tina, the owner of The Natural Grocer store in town. Stirring the honey in my tea, I contemplated whether Dad would continue taking Vitamin D after he and Tina eventually broke up. At the same time, I also stood there contemplating *how could someone as smart in school as Gwen be so dumb?*

Three knocks rapped on the front door. Holding my mug of tea, I left the kitchen and walked down the front hallway, turning to see my tousled mane of hair in the mirror on the wall, the one Dad always checked like a boxer entering the ring before he left on a date.

I opened the front door to find Gwen standing on the top concrete stair, her hair more disheveled than mine.

"Hi!" Gwen said with a huge smile on her face. Shoulders to her ears, she fast-waved bye to Andrew, who revved his junk engine and peeled out of the driveway. I figured Old Man Coleman was probably grumbling under his breath while he stared out the window. "Can I come in?" she asked, opening the screen door a crack.

"Sure," I said, without too much welcome in my voice. I wanted to say, *if you tell me you're sorry and that you've figured out that your boyfriend is no better than pond scum.*

"Is your dad home?" Gwen asked, slipping past me into the front hallway. Her makeup case peeked out between a pink sweatshirt and the side of the paisley-print bag that she dropped on the floor.

"He stayed at Tina's," I said, recalling the late-night text I got from him before I shut off Jimmy Fallon and went to bed.

"Good." She leaned over her knees in a contorted position like she had to pee or was holding something else in.

"Why?" I asked, annoyance in my voice at the fact that she seemed clueless to my feelings about last night, not to mention she hadn't even acknowledged the fight.

"I slept over Andrew's," Gwen said, right before she let out a long, high-pitched squeal that reminded me of those overly hysterical fans who scream for their favorite TikTok performers.

"Seriously?" I sat down on the edge of the sofa across from Gwen, who dramatically collapsed into my father's La-Z-Boy chair. I set my tea on the side table.

She tucked her hands under the thighs of her skinny jeans, her bony shoulders protruding out of her peach-colored T-shirt. "We did it last night!"

No words came out of my slightly opened mouth as my mind scrambled to understand.

Gwen leaned forward. "You look shocked."

The color of tainted green, that toxic way pollen coats nature in June, spread to the corners of my inner mental screen.

"I know," Gwen said, both palms raised in the air, before I had a chance to say anything. "I'm kind of in shock too. I mean, I know Andrew's the one and everything, we've been dating for practically eight months. I just wanted to be sure of the right time. Remember that night he wanted me to stay over a couple of months ago? *He* really wanted to. He told me he loved me and everything—I just didn't feel ready, which I think frustrated him. Anyway, we talked about it happening last night, so I brought my clothes after work, just in case. I told my mom I'd be with you and Frankie at the beach last night and that I slept over here, so I need you to cover for me in case she ever asks. Just like that time

I didn't tell your dad when you slept over freshman year when Livvy's guy friends slept over too. Don't forget that."

I felt a burn inside my chest. I wasn't about to give Gwen a yes or no on her request until she came to her senses. "Gwen. What the heck is going on? Are you going to talk about what happened last night, that really bad fight that your boyfriend started?"

"Oh," Gwen said, shaking her head like she was coming to from losing consciousness. "The fight. Yeah. Well, that was ridiculous. Andrew was just mad about Paul liking me for so long. It wasn't a big deal."

"It wasn't a big deal?" I asked, banging the heel of my slipper sock against the floor. "That was more than just having words with someone. Paul got his face punched in by your jealous boyfriend, and he didn't do anything to provoke the situation! Don't you think that's kind of intense?"

Gwen closed her eyes, as if I wasn't there. "I told you, Andrew gets jealous," she said. She swung her leg back and forth and then stared at the knit blanket hanging over the edge of the couch. "And he'd been drinking too, which probably made it worse. I Snapchatted Paul in the bathroom late last night at Andrew's, though, and he's okay—but Andrew doesn't know I did, so don't ever say anything about that either, okay?"

I raised my brows. "It's not like Andrew and I are buddies. You don't have to worry about that. I'm just confused, not to mention pissed, since I was searching the beach for you last night, concerned for your safety."

Gwen tilted her head. "Okay, stop. Andrew's not going to punch *me* in the face. He just doesn't want anyone looking at me.

To be honest, I kind of feel the same way. Have you seen his six-pack? But we're first loves now, so I guess I don't have to worry about anyone else. Anyway, are you going to cover for me with my mother or not?"

I stared at Gwen as she sat back against the couch, looking tired from either exhaustion from being up all night or because she had just talked herself into something she wasn't entirely sure she believed. "Nothing about this is off to you? That there's drama every time Andrew's around, or you go somewhere, or there's other guys involved—guys that don't do anything wrong?"

Gwen sighed. "I think that's how it is when you love someone and they love you too—you're protective of them. God," she added, her shoulders drooping. "You haven't even asked me about my first time."

Protective or possessive, Gwen?

A twinge of uneasiness moved through my body. I couldn't tell whether it was about Andrew and my feelings about him, or the fact that my best friend just told me she had sex for the first time and I didn't even have a boyfriend yet. "Sorry," I said, tucking my hair behind my ear, glad I didn't have to answer about covering for her yet. "So you're each other's firsts, huh?"

"Yes!" Gwen clapped her hands together as she scooted back to the edge of her seat. "I feel so happy—and sore—but in a good way."

"Sore in a good way?" I asked. "I think you need to elaborate, but spare me the details."

"Well," Gwen said, wrinkling her nose, "it sort of hurts."

I crossed my legs in my pajama bottoms. "What kind of hurt?" I asked. "Fall down on the ice and get shin bruises like we did on the bogs during middle school or achy flu hurt?"

Gwen looked up at the ceiling, one eye closed. "I'd say, weight class at the gym hurt, two days later, particularly after squats. Sore muscles, but you're glad you went."

"Gotcha," I said, twirling my ankle. I tried to appear happy for Gwen, but knowing inside, regardless of whether she gave weight to my dreams, that she had just given herself away to a complete jerk.

"It wasn't like I thought it would be, you know, firecrackers and lightning bolts or anything like that," Gwen said, twirling the end of her hair, "but I like the way our bodies fit together, kind of like a puzzle."

"Wow. You're a poet now. Are you going to tell your mom at some point at least?"

"No," Gwen said, shaking her straight, jet-black, bed-headed hair.

"Why not? She talked to you about safe sex in freaking sixth grade. You did use protection, right?" I asked.

"Yes, although I don't think it matters if we're each other's firsts. Anyway, I'm no longer a virgin, and I can't wait for you to have the same experience, so we can compare notes," Gwen said.

"I think you'll be waiting a while."

Gwen laughed. "That's yet another reason why Frankie and I love you."

I hugged my knees into my chest, trying to refrain from yelling at her about being so stupid while searching for some common ground so I could keep her close, and close the gap that seemed to be widening between us. "Actually, I did talk to someone at the beach last night."

Gwen leaned forward. "What? Who?"

"One of the cops who broke up the party."

Gwen pulled at the sock that was pushed down in her sneaker. "A friend of your dad's?"

I hugged my knees tighter. "No. That rookie cop I met last year when I told Detective Dyer about my vision involving Denise. He's taking the same class as me at the station."

Gwen leaned farther over her legs. "Stop. It. Now. I remember him when he came into Holly's last year with Len. He's *gorgeous*."

I shifted position on the couch, tucking one leg underneath me. "His name is Bobby." *As if there might be a chance.*

"Okay, so was it like oh, hi Officer Bobby, yeah, don't worry, I'm leaving the beach, see you in class? Or was it like, an actual one-on-one conversation?"

"He actually helped me try to find you and then offered me a ride home while I waited for Frankie," I said, giving her a look to let her know I was still mad about the whole thing. "Meanwhile, Frankie seems to be quite the partier these days."

Gwen slapped her hands on both legs. "I couldn't care less about Frankie at this moment! Oh my God—he offered you a ride home?"

"Yeah, but it's not like he asked me out on a date or anything. It was more of a courtesy ride."

Gwen threw her hands in the air. "Are you an idiot? He likes you!"

There's only one idiot in this room, I thought, though I tried to keep Gwen talking, thinking maybe I'd have a chance to get her to see reason before she left. "He was probably just asking because of my dad's connection to Len."

"Maybe," Gwen considered, twirling her hair around her pointy finger. "Wow, an older guy no less. Dang, girl."

I pulled my leg in closer to me on the couch, feeling the need to retreat inside myself. "I don't know how old he is, or if he's even available. I'm not interested in that right now anyway." *Since I can't think of anything else except my dream and how stupid you're being about this kid.*

"He can't be that much older. Maybe he took the police exam right out of high school. You'll be eighteen in December, so that's not such a big deal," Gwen said. She yawned and stretched her arms over her head until she touched the wall behind my father's chair. "Age doesn't matter the older you get anyway."

"Um, in my father's eyes it might."

"Well, no one's going to pass your dad's test. The guy could be twelve. Anyway, I better get home so my mom doesn't get all suss. Livvy and I are supposed to go to the mall while she's home from college for the weekend. Do you want to come?" Gwen rose from the chair.

"No thanks," I said, my heart racing in my chest, knowing Gwen was going to ask for my final answer on whether or not I'd cover for her.

"Well, can I count on you or not?" Gwen crossed her arms over her chest. "Cause there's plenty of times I've covered for you, like that other time when we prank called one of your dad's girlfriends and we lied when he asked if it was us. Remember that, in fifth grade? Cause I do."

I stared at a spot on the floor, hesitating a moment. "Just tell me, please tell me, that you at least know it wasn't nothing that happened last night and that you know deep down inside that it was a way bigger deal than you're making it out to be, and probably why you want me to cover for you, if you're being totally honest."

Gwen picked up her bag with two hands in the front hall. "Would you seriously out me to my mother? There's fights at the beach every weekend, Devon, you're just not there to see them."

I felt my cheeks sting, even though I didn't go to parties by choice. "It's just that it's more serious now that you've had sex. I don't want you to get hurt."

Gwen stomped her foot on the floor. "Would you stop worrying about me? I told you, your dreams are wrong, the fight was no big deal, and I already texted Paul to make sure he was all right. Besides, Andrew promised me he'd stop thinking I'd cheat on him after we slept together, cause then he'd know for sure that we're for real."

I flinched back on the couch. "Hold on. He bribed you to have sex with him?"

"He didn't *bribe* me," Gwen said, rolling her eyes like I had no clue about boyfriend and girlfriend behavior. "It was more like how you and I drew blood from our fingers in second grade and made each other promise we'd always be best friends, remember?"

I felt trapped in another time frame. "I remember, Gwen, I just don't think it's the same thing." My heart pounded in my chest as Gwen picked up her bag in the front hall and swung it over her shoulder to leave. "I just hope you didn't make a mistake, that's all I'm saying."

Gwen paused. "What's all this Debbie Downer crap? Do you honestly want to rain on my parade? Can you just let me be happy?"

Guilt seeped into my pores.

"Look," Gwen sighed. "Do you have my back or not?"

I bit my lip, in the same place I had already caused a tear. "Yeah, sure, I have your back. I won't say anything to your mom if she asks."

Gwen sighed in exasperation. "Thank you. I'll head out through the back."

I listened to Gwen leave through the kitchen slider doors, toward the path connecting our streets.

But I couldn't—no, I wouldn't—stop worrying, about something that felt so off to me, regardless of whether Gwen knew it or not.

CHAPTER TEN

The following Thursday night, noticing the way my heart beat in excitement every time I stepped into the workshop conference room, I realized how happy I felt here—happier at the local police station than I did anywhere else, except maybe being home alone.

"Did you find your friend?" Bobby asked, sitting down beside me at the table before class started.

"Oh. Yeah, thanks," I said. I averted my gaze since the dark circles under my eyes were hard to ignore. *But I lost her again,* I wanted to say, wishing I could tell him that if I didn't have my best friend and her boyfriend dominating my mind, keeping me up at night, that I would have liked to have talked to him more at the beach. Or anywhere outside of class, since I felt way more drawn to Bobby than kids in my class at Hanley High School.

Instead, I chewed the inside of my mouth, saying a silent prayer to Gram that I did well in the remote viewing exercises scheduled for tonight. I had to do well. We only had one more class to go, which meant one more chance for me to prove myself to these professionals that I had some skill.

"All right," Allison began. She looked almost as tired as me in her buttoned-up blouse. "As we discussed last week, we will be working on an actual, previously solved case that occurred in a different state and has been approved for educational purposes. Tonight your "job" is to locate where someone's ex-husband, who was in contempt of court, might be hiding. Shall we get to it?"

My pulse quickened.

Help me prove I have something, Gram, God, and whoever else might be listening. Something I can use at will, when I need to, not just when I'm asleep. Please. Let me find this guy.

Allison flipped off the overhead light, without providing any additional details, and led the fifteen of us through the regular weekly meditation to quiet our minds. After we sat in silence for five minutes, which hadn't relaxed me one bit, Allison, in that firm voice—prompting navy blue colors to come to my mind that made me wonder if her career was what caused her marriage to fail—said, "You may begin to identify the location of Target 45."

My heart lurched into my throat, as if a gun had gone off before a fifty-yard sprint. I rubbed my tired eyes. *I will not leave this class tonight without some kind of success.*

"Tune in to the visual data that may arise in your minds," Allison said, at the front of the room. "Focus on your third eye, that space between your eyebrows, otherwise known as one's second sight. Make mental notes of whether you feel or hear anything in that space that might be used as data, even using your olfactory senses to 'smell' anything that may have significance, all the while opening to whatever information wants to come in, in whatever way it can."

I twitched my feet under the table. *Smell?* The smell of McDonald's hamburgers immediately entered my mind, or nostrils. How could you tell if someone had really grabbed fast food for dinner, and if I literally smelled hamburgers and fries, or I was imagining things? How could you smell something that wasn't really there?

"Now, with your eyes still closed, as if you are standing in the center of your mind's eye, look to your right," Allison said, "Make note of what you see. Next, look left, observing the view in the opposite direction. Take a moment. Now, without moving your head physically, imagine looking behind you, as if you are actually turning your head. Trust what you see."

Hank cleared his throat at the end of our row. It sounded like he had had mac and cheese for dinner. *Focus. Just get something to put down on the piece of paper, so you don't look like a fool for the third week in a row.*

Swirl formations moved throughout my body, those hot and cold weather patterns that cause tornadoes.

Do not let your anxiety take over. I pressed both feet hard into the floor. *You are not going home tonight with another fail. Show me something, God. Some detail. Please.*

Immediately, in some windshield wiper-like move, my mental screen cleared. My eyes began fluttering, rapidly, picking up speed, momentum, under my closed lids.

Then, information appeared in my mind. The exact same way it did at night when I was half asleep, like those grainy movie images on old-time movie reels. Except this time, the images were coming to me while I was awake.

I tried to contain my excitement so the images wouldn't leave. Squinting, I paid intense attention to the black-and-white details flashing before me as if my life depended on it.

What felt like only a few minutes later, a buzzer filled the small room, like an unwanted morning alarm from Allison's iPhone.

"Take a moment to write down everything you might have seen or experienced in some way," Allison said, before flicking on the lights. The intense, fluorescent glare burst through my still-closed lids.

I took another few seconds after everyone else had put down their pencils, adding one last detail that entered my mind. I felt like I was scribbling down the last word found in the game of Boggle, even after the sand timer runs out.

Bobby watched me while I wrote and then quickly glanced down at his paper. I wondered if he had gotten something too, or maybe even the same details.

The clock ticked high up on the back wall. I bounced my leg against the seat. *Maybe everyone got something intuitively and I'd be nothing special.* Well, at least I'd have participated, and given some information and, after another sleepless night, I'd consider that some kind of progress. Would it be enough, though, for Len to put me in the advanced class after this one was done? What if everyone got something? How would they choose who went on to the next class?

"Remember, let go of analyzing what you might have received," Allison said, holding the black dry-erase marker in her hand. "Your only responsibility, as a remote viewer, is to give what you get. Who in the first row wants to start?"

Against the wall, Lisa tossed her pencil down on top of her paper and sat back with attitude. "I got absolute jack squat."

"Allow for error," Allison said as she moved to the next person after writing "jack squat" on the board, prompting everyone else in the class to laugh. "Baseball players don't always hit the ball."

Ed chuckled, as if he expected everyone to fail.

"And you?" Allison asked Ed.

"Well, I did see a boat," Ed responded. "But I'm wondering if it's because I'd like to buy one to take down to the Keys when I retire."

Sitting in the chair beside him, Walter laughed out loud. "That's all right, cause I saw a porch and figured it's because it's the one in my backyard that needs fixing. I'm starting to think there's not much to this whole thing, and for some of us, we just need to stick with the left-brain smarts that've gotten us this far."

Allison smiled. "You're entitled to that perspective and certainly don't have to be part of the advanced class, Walter." The rest of the class chuckled. "Anyone else?"

I glanced at my notes, comparing mine to Ed and Walter's, whom I definitely felt wouldn't be pursuing the more advanced class once this introductory workshop was over. That offered a better chance for me.

Paula, the detective who'd been talking to Bobby during the first class, moved her cup of coffee to the right of her notes so it wouldn't spill. "I saw, or maybe I felt, I guess, based on what we've learned, a section of woods, like woods that would border a local park. Not too far in, fairly shallow, and I don't know if it makes sense or anything, since a deadbeat would probably be found somewhere more discreet."

Allison held up her finger. "No analyzing. Just give what comes."

"Right," Paula said, crossing her legs before turning to Lynette, who was next in line.

I stared at a small stain on the table in front of me, thinking about when it was my turn. Even though I had a few things come to me, what if they weren't correct? I could hear Gloria dig into her pocketbook the way she did trying to find a piece of gum. Even though the details of the information felt weighted and meaningful to *me,* it was kind of like the dreams about Andrew—I still couldn't prove he was a cheater.

"I saw a concrete building," Lynette said, scratching the back of her head while she cleared her throat. I could feel how awkward some of the people in the class felt, as if they were playing childish games with no concrete outcome.

It was the total opposite for me. I felt like people were speaking my language, and that I finally had someone to talk to, even though I also felt nervous to share what I got.

As Allison wrote Lynette's results on the whiteboard, some of the detectives, arms crossed over their chests, whispered among themselves, pointing out the common thread of outdoor data running through people's reports. Allison ignored giving feedback, staying tight-lipped. She pointed to our row next.

Bobby leaned forward, hands clasped on the table. "Tall guy with a beer belly, a horse, maybe a cowboy?" His voice cracked a little when he answered, his cheeks turning a little pink. I pictured him in high school, giving answers in Spanish class when he wasn't sure.

Allison added Bobby's impressions to the whiteboard, neither revealing nor dismissing Bobby's information, while I mentally compared Bobby's notes to my own.

Up next, my heart pounded inside my chest so hard it hurt. I hoped to God I didn't sound ridiculous sharing my findings and that Walter and Ed, and the other patronizing adults, would keep their sarcastic mouths shut.

"And you, Devon?"

A feeling ran through me, a chill of truth, as Gram used to call it. I realized right then, that in some way, these people *were* my peers now, even though no one had really gone out of their way to make me feel welcome other than Bobby and maybe Gloria. I felt more weirdly connected to them than most kids in my grade. It made me feel instantly—I realized for the first time—like I belonged.

I took a deep breath. "I saw a horse too," I said, rotating my ankle under the table, "and black boots by a doorstep on a newly shellacked porch."

Walter clapped his hands high in the air like it was Happy Hour. "That's two for the porch!"

After the laughter in the class subsided, I lifted my chin. "There was also an old pick-up in the driveway, like a '61 Chevrolet Apache. And the number 79 in black numbers on the house. Shingled."

Allison stared at me, like she was sizing me up to take my measurements. The class grew quiet. Then, she nodded in silence and simply wrote my data on the board underneath the other details.

George Flynn, a stout, burly detective in the second row turned around to face me, with no small effort. "Pretty specific, kid. I like the car reference—you're PJ Alante's kid, from the auto body shop, right?"

"Yeah," I said, wondering whether he was complimenting me on my remote viewing information or because I knew a thing or two about cars.

"How about a town, though?" Jon Furlow, one of the other detectives, chided over his bony shoulder. "Can you grab that, since it could be any porch in any town in America?"

"How about the street?" Rich Hadsley, a ruddy-faced, middle-aged guy chimed in, a guy who hadn't said boo since the class started.

I pressed my toes hard into my sandals. *Here we go.* Everyone stared at me, like I was some zoo animal on display.

"Let's go easy on our young protégé, shall we? Data will be assigned meaning later and either validated or invalidated at the end of class," Allison said. She never looked my way, which made me feel like she wasn't necessarily being nice to me, just trying to keep the class in control. "And lastly, Gloria?"

Gloria shimmied to the end of her seat, adjusting her glasses as she read from her sheet of paper. "I saw pigs, a 4 x 4 truck in the driveway, and an in-law attached to a red-and-brown wooden house. I say shingled as well, like Devon stated."

Ed let out a whistle. "Looks like the females have it today. Except for Paula and Lisa. Maybe next time, ladies."

Allison put the cap back on the dry-erase marker. "Thank you for sharing, everyone. Please turn in your written findings at the end of your row. Feedback will be given at the end of class. Now, let's move on to our partner exercise. This will be the preferred method of working at the department, if remote viewing is used as a tool that is when, after next week, you will no longer have me as a guide."

Bobby and I slid our sheets of paper toward Hank. Allison collected and organized each table's data and put the stack of paper inside a manila envelope that she slid under her laptop. Someone cracked open a can of Pepsi. I hoped Allison would match me with Bobby. Instead, though, a few moments later, I was assigned to working with Gloria.

"Well done, girl," Gloria said, scooting her chair closer to mine.

"Thanks, but we don't know the facts yet." I looked over at the closed envelope on the desk.

"That's true," Gloria said. Then, she raised a finger in the air. "But the specifics, the way you delivered them, that's good work. Good practice."

I cracked my knuckles. "So, you've done this work before, as a medium?"

"Twenty years, many departments. Always good to stay up on classes, though, to brush up on skills."

"How did you start, if you don't mind me asking?" I said.

"Don't mind at all. Wish someone had explained how this works to me too, early in my career. Had so much in my head, nearly drove me crazy. Bad accidents, homicides . . . you name it, I saw it in my head. Victims who passed—they came to me, in spirit. Nonstop. Things started happening after a car accident I had thirty-five years ago. I finally said to myself, 'Gloria, if you don't give this over to the police, you're going to bust.' I had a few evidential cases, built my reputation in a few local departments, and then they started calling after that. You know, sporadically over the years at first. Now, though, they call on a fairly regular basis. I work a regular job too, dear, clerical work, at a local town hall. This is something I do on the side, though I have to say, it does takes up quite a bit of time and energy, especially the way the world is today."

"Sounds intense," I said, trying not to show the anxiety I felt inside my body at practically everything Gloria was saying, along with wanting to know if I got anything solid in the exercise, which might mean I had a better chance of being right about Andrew and getting my best friend back. I had so many questions. "You started communicating with people after you had an accident?"

"Yes. A year before I had my first child. Never looked back. Okay, ready to do some work?" Gloria wrote her target information on a small piece of paper and folded it in half as Allison had instructed earlier. "We'll call the project Target 'K.' Now, take some deep breaths, get centered and then try to identify the person, place, or thing I wrote down on my paper."

I closed my eyes. I felt like the time I had stood at the end of the diving board at the YMCA and someone yelled, "Go already!" expecting me to just jump the way the other kids did, which made me want to flip them the finger, even though I was only seven. This time, though, I took a deep inhale. I knew I wasn't going to turn around and step off the board.

I held my hands in my lap, palms up, the backs of my thighs pressed against the chilly air-conditioned chair. A thought dashed across my mind, like a hummingbird. I wondered if Gloria would have the ability to connect with Gram or my mother. Was that the kind of thing you could just ask a medium when she wasn't officially on the clock?

A phone sounded in someone's pants pocket, *Plush* by Stone Temple Pilots, a song I recalled my mom listening to when I was little. I started to think about what my mom might think, about me being here, in a class like this. Would she have thought it was weird? Maybe she'd find it interesting. A few seconds later, after someone scratched and scrunched things around in their backpack, the room gradually returned to stillness.

"Minor distractions," Gloria said. She rotated the ring on her hand as if this was all in a day's work. "Just refocus, dear."

I took another breath, attempting to block out the quiet murmur in the room as the other groups practiced among themselves. With only black on my mental screen, I sat in quiet anticipation of receiving whatever data might be revealed about Target "K."

My mind wandered again. Thoughts about the previous case, how we'd find out soon how we did in front of the whole class. If I did well, then maybe I might be able to focus my mind deliberately on finding more details out about Andrew. Like maybe find out if he'd already been with that girl with the belly ring, and if it hadn't already happened, then how to find out when it might.

If I could focus my thoughts.

Just then, an image of a man jumped into my mind. It was as if I was walking down an alley and he just appeared, out of nowhere. *But somewhere.* A shadowy, see-through nylon-type silhouette stood against a backdrop of darkness. The details, though fairly visual, came to me more in a feeling: The man's hair receded past his forehead, his t-shirt white, V-neck, his job as a grocer, no, a chef perhaps, hair dark, wet, maybe Greek in ethnicity. The information flowed fast and furious, like the current on a river during a white-water rafting trip—feelings, connected to images, some of the data flickering in almost dark pixel formation, as if formulating at my request.

My eyelids fluttered like the wings of that hummingbird.

"Slow it down," Gloria guided me in a hushed, yet powerful tone, as the other partners shared their readings. "Tell the information to slow down."

Could she read my mind or did she know I got something by the way my eyelids moved?

I squeezed my hands together, attempting to get a grip on the current of my racing thoughts. The man's face was revealed more clearly this time. He looked to be 70ish. Retired, yet still working. Then, without warning, he clutched the V-neck part of his grease-stained T-shirt, the stains representing years of hard labor.

My own chest suddenly grew heavy, as if something forceful pressed against me. The sensation threatened to block my air. Instinctively, I opened my eyes, my hand clutching at the fabric of my shirt around my heart.

Gloria stared at me with an expression that was hard to decipher. Did she think I was being dramatic?

I took a few quiet breaths in through my nose, becoming more aware of the room, yet still feeling somewhat in that other place.

A quiet, puffy pause sat suspended in the space between Gloria and me like insulation foam. I observed the lines in her aging forehead, little narrow speed bumps, as the other partners spoke among themselves in the background, joking about their strange findings.

"It's like that sometimes—intense, especially in the beginning," Gloria said. "Just tell it to slow down whenever it goes too fast. Remember, you're the one in control. Just like a new, rambunctious puppy, it needs to be told what to do."

It. Tell *it* to slow down.

Who or what was *it* anyway? I stared at the baseboard behind Gloria's chair until the sections blurred. The information, the *it,* came toward me so fast in my dreams at night, in my visions, it was as if it traveled at the speed of light—toward *me,* the intended destination for some reason.

Was there really a way to control what I saw? Could I really tell *it* to slow down so I could see even more detail?

"Well?" Gloria asked, crossing one leg over the other. "Are you going to tell me what you got?"

If I got things right with Gloria, and if I got at least one thing right in the already-solved case Allison gave us to work with, then tonight would be a win. And if I won here, then I'd feel better about my dream and the idea that I'd definitely have a better shot of getting Gwen to break up with Andrew before he had the opportunity to cause any more chaos.

"Of course," I said, blinking to clear my thoughts from my overtired brain. I proceeded to tell Gloria everything I saw about the man that appeared in my head.

Gloria only nodded once, similar to how Judge Judy might before deciding someone's fate. Then, keeping her eyes on me the entire time, she said, "You got it, girl. You got my father. Owner of a grocery store, a Lebanese grocery store more specifically, and being specific is crucial for intuitive work. His name was Kuri, hence Target 'K.' Good work."

I recalled the heaviness I felt in my chest during the exercise. "Is your dad okay?"

"Of course he's not okay," she said. "He's dead. Well, he's okay now . . . ."

I gritted my teeth. "Sorry. I didn't know what it meant. I wasn't sure if he was alive or not."

Gloria winked and then continued, "You intuitively experienced the heart attack that took his life. That's good, accurate work."

The conversations rose in volume at the front of the room. "You seem so okay with it," I half-heartedly laughed. It was hard for me to think about Gram or my mother for too long without feeling sadness, and sometimes anger at my mother.

"It's the circle of life," Gloria said, rubbing hand cream on her aging hands. "Though he's my papa and I loved him, I've done so many readings for people, I've come to believe in something bigger—that he's with me, here," Gloria pointed to her heart, "and here," she added, gesturing to the larger space around her body and the room. "They say the spiritual realm is only three feet away, past the ethereal body—that our loved ones are with us all the time, guiding us and continuing to take part in our lives."

A chill ran through me, causing me to sit upright. Gram had always taught me that Mom showed us she was still here through signs. That's how I knew Gram was still watching over me, especially whenever a cardinal appeared. That's what always brought me comfort in the sadness.

I reached for my necklace, rubbed the grooves of the dragonfly's wings between my fingers. This was the first time, though, I had ever heard that our loved ones could exist in the space around us, like *really be right there*, the way I thought I saw Mom last year in my room in the middle of the night, right before Dad took me to the hospital to get evaluated, and getting me a prescription for Ativan—medication I refused to take.

I looked over at Walter, who laughed about something not related to work with his partner. I wanted to ask Gloria if the rules were the same for people who died naturally versus those who took their life on purpose—was *everyone* in spirit *right there?* Were the rules different for my mother?

Gloria dropped the crème in her large purse and sat back in her seat. "Now, since we have a couple minutes, tell me, dear, what's going on with your friend."

"What?" I asked. I looked over at Bobby, who sat conversing with Lisa in the second row.

"Not that friend," Gloria smiled, one bottom tooth slightly crooked, which, in my opinion, added to her charm. "I'm sensing a girlfriend of yours isn't exercising the best choices, shall we say, in her male companions."

My pulse raced. If Gloria knew that, could she also tell me what to do about the whole Andrew thing? I uncrossed and then crossed my ankles, making an awkward slapping sound with my feet against the rung of the chair. "My best friend isn't dating the best guy. But how did you know that?"

"It's a concern of yours and I picked it up in your energy field," Gloria said. "You've spoken to this friend about your concerns?"

I heard Ed obnoxiously laugh in the background— those people who don't care about anyone else when their work is finished. "Yes," I answered, keeping my response to a minimum, one to respect Gwen's privacy since I didn't know Gloria any more than I knew anyone else in the room and also because I wanted to see if she could give me more without my specifically asking for it.

"Well, then, you said your peace. It's your friend's right to choose her dating partners. Some people don't want the information, my dear, you have to remember that as a working intuitive. She might want to watch her back, though. That's what I'm getting, anyway. Young love, sometimes . . . so foolish."

I took a deep breath, hooking my feet around the legs of the chair. There was no way I'd let Gwen get hurt. Not on my watch, anyway. But if Gwen didn't want the information, which she certainly didn't seem to, how could I prevent anything bad from happening? I couldn't possibly let this go, my body wouldn't let me—the dreams kept coming without my wanting them to. Didn't that mean I had a responsibility to do something, to keep doing something, to get Gwen to see?

When Allison had us return to our regular seats so we could learn the results about the guy in contempt of court, thoughts bombarded my brain of how I might be able to share what Gloria said with Gwen. But then the thought came that even though Gwen used to love hearing about my dreams and how I was taking this class to advance myself, now that the dreams involved *her* as the main character, she might dismiss what Gloria said, too, as some medium weirdo who didn't even know her or anything about her life.

Allison wrote across the board, this time in red. I could hear George Flynn's labored breathing in the first row, the class as quiet as the time we watched the first 9/11 documentary in school.

"Holy cow," George said as the words became visible.

Forty-five-year-old male, with dark receding hairline, a mustache, weighing 240 pounds, standing 6'3", found hidden in a farmhouse on a stretch of land that included a horse barn and cattle.

"Hey," Paula said, sitting up straighter in the front row. "I said the woods. That sort of indicates woods, I think."

Bobby elbowed me gently in my arm, before he leaned in and whispered, "How 'bout them horses?"

My mouth felt dry. At least I nailed the horse detail, and maybe even the guy, since I saw boots and a pick-up truck, which I guess indicated a guy, even if I was kind of stereotyping.

"Too bad the state's withheld information to protect the person's privacy, otherwise we could validate the address for the high-schooler back there," Walter said, pointing his thumb over his shoulder at me.

Allison picked up her thermos. "You're right, it's too bad," she said, before taking a sip. "However, I can tell you, the number of the house was 79."

Every single adult in the two rows in front of me turned around in their seats.

"Nice job, girl," Gloria said, slapping the table behind me like she had hit the slot machines at Foxwoods.

Hank leaned closer to high-five me, stating in a matter-of-fact tone, "Now that's a hit."

My body felt light, something rising up inside of me. I recalled feeling the exact same way when Len validated my information on Denise's case—the only other time in my whole life I had ever felt this way.

"Great way to end class tonight, everybody," Allison said, shutting down her laptop. "Though the ultimate purpose of this workshop is learning how to be of service in the field, it's also important to know for our egos when we get a hit. Validation is everything. I'll see you next week for the final class."

I sat on my hands, realizing that even though Allison never smiled at me or congratulated me personally, she gave me credit. Watching the others get up to leave, I stayed seated for another minute, my insides tangled up like those beach roses on the Cape—a perfectly imperfect twisted entanglement of pink buds you'd never even want to try to pry apart.

I took a deep breath and then exhaled, nice and slow, the way we learned in meditation. I couldn't remember ever feeling this happy, or hopeful, despite everything that had happened in my life.

Then, I remembered Gwen—and what had yet to happen, and what I knew would. What I knew with certainty would. My head throbbed over my left eye, the stress and pain and tiredness returning to me in an instant.

There was no way I could listen to Gloria's advice and let things go.

Now that I knew I could focus my mind, on purpose, to get information— information that proved accurate in my waking state—I couldn't leave it up to Gwen to figure things out on her own.

A nervous feeling moved in my stomach. I had waited too long to help Denise last year. I'd regret that for the rest of my life. I wasn't about to make the same mistake with my best friend.

CHAPTER ELEVEN

Three days later, on Sunday morning of the long Memorial Day weekend, I opened my eyes to the bright sun streaming in through my bedroom palladium windows. I rolled on my side, avoiding the harsh light, feeling like a vampire. A vampire who had stayed up into the early hours of Friday and Saturday night trying to connect with *that thing*, the *it*, the way I had in class, to get something else on Andrew, on purpose—this time with no results.

I stretched the covers over my head. How had my intuition been spot on during class *twice*, and yet when I came home and tried to connect on more personal matters, I didn't get a thing? I didn't even dream. I asked for one. I prayed. I requested some kind of other specific detail that proved my dream about Andrew was right, and yet, nothing. How could I use my intuition at will if it didn't come through on a consistent basis? Did it only work because I had someone to guide the process, first Allison as the teacher and then Gloria as my partner during the second exercise?

For another hour or so I stayed in bed, drifting in and out of broken sleep due to the annoying lawn mower of some early riser on our street. I pulled the covers closer to my eyes to deepen the darkness, thinking about something else Allison said during class, about being an empath—someone who feels other people's emotions to such a degree that you can pick up on their pain. That's how I felt doing the remote viewing about Gloria's dad—feeling his heart attack as if it was happening to me.

Allison had said that children, particularly highly sensitive ones, often start out this way, something about being closer to that "other realm" when they're young. That they often lose those natural-born skills by the time they're seven or eight years old, due to entering the social-development phase, where imaginary friends cease to be and real-life friends—and other people's judgments—enter the scene. I slid my foot outside my covers to find some air, remembering that's how I used to feel, a lot of the time, when I was little.

I had always been the one who needed to feed the birds on the back deck, because I couldn't stand the pit in my stomach if I had food on my plate and the feeder was empty. I used to imagine a mother bird going out to get food and then not finding any to bring back to her family. It was like I couldn't eat if I knew someone else, especially the birds, had no food. I even told Dad once that I didn't want him to kill a spider on the windshield of our car with his windshield wipers because what if the spider's parents came looking for him and he was gone?

I pulled my foot back underneath the covers. I remembered how Dad had laughed, telling me to toughen up and that spiders don't have families. I never talked to him again about my feelings about bugs, or birds, or animals without families in shelters that used to send me almost into a panic. Never mind not bothering to ask him if he ever read *Charlotte's Web,* for that matter. But I never killed a bug whenever I saw them in private.

Outwardly, though, I developed a cool exterior. As if I had deliberately let go of that sensitive part of me, without realizing it. Or maybe I did realize it, I simply didn't allow myself to feel what I had lost.

Until this class.

I pulled the comforter off my face and lay on my back, listening to the stop and start of the mower and the cars driving past on their way to wherever they were going to likely have fun on Memorial Day weekend. It came to me now that I had never liked anyone being hurt. Not just animals. I could feel someone's pain so intensely I couldn't physically stand the feelings I felt in my own body.

A feeling of release reverberated around me—I imagined someone letting go of a rope that had been coiled about my body, holding me tight to myself. I turned toward the window, the thin sheets still covering my face. Now that I thought more about it, a lot of times that's why I would pick at my skin, making pock marks in my arm, as if I was creating an opening to let myself out of some kind of personal prison. Whether myself or someone else's.

A police cruiser sailed past the house, the sirens loud and then fading in the distance. There was another time when this had happened. In fifth grade, when Avo told Dad, Uncle Rob, and me at supper one night about a family in a neighboring town that lost their home in a fire. I couldn't fall asleep for a week because I worried about "the kids having no roof over their heads, no clothes, can you imagine such a thing." Never mind how I felt when kids sat alone at the lunch table at school. I always attempted some kind of pursed, closed-mouth smile to let those misfit-feeling kids know that even though I had Gwen and Frankie, and it might have looked like we had it all together and were considered somewhat cool, I felt what they felt more than they could possibly know: That most of the time I felt alone too, and privately anxious, even when I was around a swarm of people. Maybe even more.

When Avo told us about the house fire, Dad got up to clear his plate, which is when he saw me sticking the prongs of my fork hard into my palm. "What the hell are you doing?" he snapped. My face had burned so red, so hot, that I thought I might explode—from the humiliation, yes, but also from the feelings of being so very different from my family.

I saw the embarrassment in Avo's eyes when she took me aside later and reprimanded me, saying, "You mustn't do that to yourself. Only people who have problems do that sort of thing." She made me promise I wouldn't do it again, and I didn't—at least not in front of anyone.

When I was alone, though, I pinched myself even harder.

It made me feel powerful. It was a twisted, no-one-tells-me-what-to-do kind of thing. My small way of saying eff you to my family and so what if my quirky habits embarrassed them. Even though I felt guilty about it at the same time. I loved my grandmother and my father for everything they had done to raise me as normal as I could be, after my mom died. I mean, I guess I turned out pretty good, considering. I had anxiety and everything, and sometimes I felt angry when I let myself think about it, but otherwise, I was a pretty regular kid. Except for my dreams.

After I left the table that night, Avo said, "She got the compassion gene from her mother." To which Dad replied, "Too much compassion is for weak people."

I didn't feel like a weak person. I didn't present like some Nervous Nellie or anything. My anxiety was more kept inside, for myself. Maybe I *was* weak, though, which made me feel more like a black sheep in the Alante family with all of their no nonsense, no drama, no emotions whatsoever.

I pushed the sheets off me, kicked all the covers farther down to the foot of my bed and stared at the plaster swirls in the ceiling. I had always felt things. That part was true. I wondered if my mom, who also struggled with anxiety, and who was the other half of my family, felt things like this, too.

My phone sounded, signaling a FaceTime call from someone. I rolled over, grabbed my phone off the side table, and saw Frankie's name running across my screen.

"Dude, you up?" He peered closer to the screen. "Duuuddde. You're looking harsh. You look like I did last night after the party at Joe Bosco's house, except not for the same reason. Let me guess—nightmares?"

I rested my head on my arm. "I actually wish I did have a nightmare, so I could have more information on Andrew."

Frankie shook his head. "Now we're looking to have nightmares? I don't get you sometimes, my friend. Why try so hard? You can get more information on Andrew today at the pool *partay* we've been waiting for, since Kristina and Doug are down at the Cape. What time are you going to Gwen's?"

I closed my eyes, the reminder of the planned *partay* I had totally forgotten about, along with the thought of Gwen being the gracious host and Andrew showing his friends around the pool in the role of playing house, definitely not on my agenda.

"You there?" Frankie asked, one eye close to the screen.

"I'm here," I said, reluctantly opening my eyes. "I'm going to pass on this one. Been there, done that whole thing."

"Yeah, but this time Sophia Prisco might be going, who happens to be Andrew's ex, who he happened to have Snapchatted this weekend. But you didn't hear that from me."

I sat up farther on my elbow, thinking back to my dream. "Does she have blond hair and a belly ring?"

"Dark brown and not sure on the hoop, but I wish I was. Do your dreams always have to be literal? Besides, just knowing she's hot means Gwen must be extra pissed. Snapping her doesn't mean Gaston cheated, per se, but it definitely caused trouble in paradise, according to my trusted sources. So, if you don't go, you could miss being on the front lines of their potential breakup."

I sighed, got out of bed, and a half hour later met Frankie at the end of the path in a T-shirt, shorts, and headband. "Is there anything else you can tell me?" I asked. The hot, early afternoon sun shone directly overhead as we walked together toward the end of the street. "You know, anything that might prove my dream is right?"

Fifteen cars filled the cul-de-sac, making me wonder just how many people Gwen had invited, and if the neighbors might question whether Gwen's parents were home.

"Just that Gwen never told either of us about her boyfriend contacting his ex," Frankie said, shoving a piece of licorice in his mouth that had been stuffed in the side of his shorts. "Which translates to the notion that she's embarrassed, since supposedly, they're so 'in love.'"

And since they've had sex, but I knew Frankie wasn't privy to that information.

"Who knows, maybe today will be the day that Gwen wakes up and smells the mighty macchiato," Frankie said, before offering me a lint-covered piece of licorice.

Music blared from the Davidsons' backyard, while the Morgans' dog barked from their front stoop next door.

I followed Frankie as he scuffed down the driveway and to the backyard of the Davidsons' colonial, to the pool area where fifty or so kids stood around the blue and gray concrete, drinking from red plastic cups. The music played at a decibel higher than Kristina and Doug would have ever allowed, considering some of the elderly neighbors living on the cul-de-sac.

Guys aggressively dunked each other in the pool, while girls in bikini tops and shorts egged them on in the deep end. *I don't even know these people,* I thought, while Frankie and I headed up the long set of wooden stairs leading to the kitchen. Hearing their laughter, I recalled Kristina's pool policy when we were younger: No one was allowed in unless an adult was present.

I wondered if she might consider applying the same rule to this crowd now.

Justin Elliot, an alcoholic Hanley High football player, sat on the ledge of the upper deck. He jumped down with a *thud* and high-fived Frankie before shoving a red cup into his hand. I heard Gwen bark from the kitchen that if anyone got one drop of beer on the floor, she was kicking them out.

I stared at Frankie's cup filled with some kind of urine-colored drink that wasn't beer. "Seriously?" I asked.

"Don't worry," Frankie said under his breath as we stepped inside the house. We came face-to-face with a swarm of girls coming back from the bathroom, who dripped water across the kitchen floor from their skimpy bikinis. "I wouldn't get drunk in the Davidsons' house. This is just to keep my reputation."

"Which is?" I asked. I watched Gwen put out another plate of freshly baked cookies like the perfect hostess before going back and cleaning a few dishes while she chatted with Andrew and his friends beside the sink. Noticing her furrowed brow, I wondered whether Gwen was stressed out about the party or about the whole Snapchatting incident. Instantly, a message arrived inside my mind. More of a feeling, a gray and black weight dropped down inside me, heavy like one of those large obsidian rocks we learned about in geology. The message was that for Gwen, the stress involved both of those things, and that more stress was on the way.

Andrew, in his stupid Vineyard Vines bathing suit, glanced in my direction, almost flaunting it in my face, that the party was packed with all his friends. As if he owned the place, even though I pretty much grew up in this house, and even though he barely looked in Gwen's parents' direction when he was around them, like someone with something to hide.

"Hey, guys," Gwen said, coming over but avoiding looking at Frankie or me directly in the face. Beckett saw us and trotted over behind Gwen, wagging his tail.

"Some party you got here," I said, reaching down to scratch the dog's fur.

Frankie started up a conversation with Nolan Murphy near the slider doors, a football goon who coaxed him outside to drink with the other players.

"Ugh," Gwen said, taking inventory of the people coming in and out of the house in their wet bathing suits. She took a towel off the island and wiped the floor.

Andrew slapped his thigh twice, causing the dog to turn and leave my side. "Want me to take Beckett out, babe?"

I stared at Andrew for a moment, watching the flash of satisfaction cross his face as if he had one-upped me with the dog. It made me wonder if Gwen told him about my dream and that I had caught him cheating. Had he made this some sick competition between us?

"Thanks, hon," Gwen said, playing the part as Andrew took Beckett outside. She laid the soggy towel over the back of one of the island chairs. With her tired face, though, Gwen looked more the part of a mother of a teenager having a pool party than a teenager having fun while her parents were down at the Cape.

I cringed. The fact that Gwen didn't even notice Andrew's manipulative tactic toward me made my stomach tie in a knot. It made me feel, after all these months, that she was under some type of dark, magic spell. Crawling out of my skin, part of me wanted to give Andrew, who sneered at me over his shoulder like a spoiled, entitled brat before he went down the stairs, the finger.

There was another part of me, though. The one that observed a rising gray mist inside my mind: A mist that gave way, magician style, to a message about Andrew being the kind of guy that explodes frogs just for fun. The message caused a stirring inside of me, a foreboding that we were dealing with someone who kept a steady supply of anger under the surface, and that he could, *would*, use it any time he deemed appropriate. Any time things didn't go his way. Though the information concerned me—and I wanted to tell Gwen to run for the hills right then and there—I kept myself steady, cool, classic Alante style.

"I actually didn't know so many people would be here," Gwen sighed. "I mean, the girls from tennis and their boyfriends, yeah, but Andrew invited so many of his friends. Well. There's nothing I can do about it now. Let's go outside with everyone else." She glanced around the kitchen in a quick attempt to keep things in order and then hurried outside, no doubt to keep an eye on Andrew's whereabouts.

"Is everything all right?" I asked. I followed a nervous-looking Gwen past the guys chugging beers on the deck and down the twenty-two stairs to the pool area where now even more teenagers stood around drinking, though only a handful of kids were from Hanley.

"Yeah, why?" Gwen said, trying to act like she wasn't going to get in big trouble if the neighbors told her parents what went down while they were away.

I knew then that she wasn't going to tell me about the Snapchatting thing. Maybe that part of our friendship, the part where we told each other everything, had changed.

"Holy shit," Gwen said. She held her right hand up to stop me in my tracks on the granite area surrounding the outdoor kitchen. "I don't believe she had the nerve to come to my house."

"Who?" I asked. I connected Gwen's stare to a group of dark-tanned girls talking and flirting with Andrew while they swooned over Beckett on the other side of the pool. One of the girls, with long dark hair and a body that looked like she worked out at the gym every day doing squats, stood particularly close to Andrew.

"Oh my God, I can't, she can't stay here, I can't believe she showed up here," Gwen said frantically under her breath, more to herself than to me.

"What? Who are you talking about?" I asked, feigning innocence, eyeing the girl who looked nothing like the girl in my dream, which could either mean that the dream wasn't literal, like Frankie suggested, or there was still some other girl Andrew planned on cheating with.

Glancing at her ribbed pink tank top, I secretly hoped the girl decided to go swimming so I could see if she had a hoop belly ring.

"Who invited you here?" Gwen asked in a raised voice. She walked around the pool with her arms crossed over her chest.

"I heard about it. I thought it was an open invitation," the girl said with a nod to Andrew. She flexed her muscular legs for all to see, reminding me of one of Dad's former hook-ups, who arrived, unwelcome, to one of the Alante cookouts. I knew, while the girl stood twirling the ends of her beach-wavy hair with her fingers, that she was the kind of person who takes advantage of a situation, even when the situation is negative.

"Did you invite her?" Gwen asked, turning to Andrew. Her voice rose in pitch, competing with the guys and girls playing water games in the turquoise-colored pool. I could see how hard Gwen tried to keep her lips from trembling.

"What are you talking about?" Andrew asked. With his small eyes honing in on Gwen, he suggested, in that typical manipulative way he had, that he was the one being offended. "I invited some kids from Marshton—I can't control who shows up when they hear about a party."

The girl looked at Andrew first and then over at her friends with a smirk. Maybe she *was* the girl in the dream. I stepped closer to the lounge chair area, trying to focus my mind on getting her to scratch her stomach.

A few feet away, Gwen squeezed her hands together, tight, while remaining silent.

Did she honestly think Andrew had a valid point? That he had nothing to do with his apparent ex-girlfriend now standing around the pool at his current girlfriend's house?

I searched for Frankie, to see if he felt the same way I did about our normally in-your-face friend, who now appeared to be at a complete loss for words.

Frankie didn't catch my eye, though; he continued sipping from the red cup as he stood talking to the only guy left from Hanley. I wondered if the small amount—or whatever amount of alcohol he was drinking—had already begun influencing his rational brain.

Gripping Beckett's leash, Andrew leaned closer to Gwen and said in a low tone, "Babe, you told me to invite my friends."

A feeling came to me then, of a hypnotist swaying a pendulum back and forth in front of someone's face—how they do that when they're trying to get a person to do something, or think something, they wouldn't normally believe.

"It's not *my* fault," he continued. The group of Marshton guys cheered and yelled, playing beer pong across the table.

My throat burned. Andrew acted so cocky, so sure of himself, like he had convinced himself of his apparent lies. The girl had obviously shown up to prove a point—and she could leave now that she had. Worse, though, was that Gwen—standing there in disbelief, humiliation, or both—looked like some helpless wimp, someone we might have gossiped about up in the tree house under different circumstances. Someone whom Gwen would have said, had she been in the position of judging someone else's relationship, "Needed to grow a spine." This girl in front me, though? I didn't know her. Gwen resembled nothing like the person I had always known her to be.

"I didn't say it was your fault," Gwen said, twitching her toes. I noticed guests began quieting their conversations in and around the pool, fully bearing witness to the unfolding drama. "It's just, i-it's my house."

"And I didn't do anything wrong to your house," Andrew said in a condescending tone. He let go of Beckett's leash in a way that made the dog seem like a burden. "She must have found out and just showed up, that's all. What do you want me to do?"

Frankie stepped beside me, next to one of the lounge chairs beside the pool, brushing my shoulder with his own. "Told you there was trouble in paradise," he whispered. "That's Sophia Prisco, if you haven't figured it out on your own, Ms. Psychic Detective. Maybe your dream was right and you got your girl."

Sophia grabbed the neon orange towel she had laid on a lounge chair with her long purple fingernails. She tossed it over one shoulder, her tank top remaining in place. "Reason 145 I'm not going out with you anymore," she said to Andrew, then gestured to her friends to leave. The guys playing beer pong halted their conversations as they stared. Cardi B on the surround-sound speakers was the only voice to be heard.

"Whatever," Andrew called after her. "You wish you were still my girlfriend."

Sophia dropped her head back and laughed. Then she turned and pulled up her tank top, revealing large breasts hanging out of her skimpy bikini top. No belly ring to be seen. "Here, have your last Snap," she said, with her friends laughing in tow as they left through the open gate.

"Nice, Sophia, classy," Andrew yelled.

Gwen closed her eyes as she stood near the edge of the pool. The sound of Andrew saying the girl's name I knew was too much for her to bear, never mind the embarrassment of being betrayed in her own backyard.

I felt a tightening in my chest as I watched Gwen wring her hands, working up the courage to speak, a characteristic she had never before been afraid to bring forth. Finally, with her lip quivering, she asked, "Why would you do that to me? Why would you invite her here?"

Andrew turned away from her, taking off his shirt like he planned to go for a casual dip in the pool. This was after he had given his posse, staring at him from the pool, a hard stare, the message that they should just go back to swimming and mind their own business. "Stop making a big deal out of everything," he said out the side of his mouth. "I used to go out with her. Obviously, I don't anymore. Relax."

Gwen lifted her chin in an attempt to be brave, no doubt feeling a bit better as everyone resumed their conversations, puppets on the end of Andrew's string. I didn't know how Andrew had suddenly become king over the Davidsons' backyard. "So you Snapped her, then?"

Andrew grabbed a cookie off one of the little tables, ignoring the chuckles of his friends finishing up their game. He took a few bites of the cookie and tossed the rest to Beckett lying in the grass. "Don't listen to Sophia. She's just pissed I broke up with her."

Gwen followed him to the table. "But did you or did you not Snapchat her? And please don't give Beckett cookies; chocolate is bad for dogs."

I held my fist to my mouth. *Yes, girl, that's the Gwen we know and love.* I figured maybe Gwen felt more confident now that Sophia left and most everyone from Hanley had gone, except for Frankie and me.

"Gwen," Andrew said, placing his large hands on her tiny shoulders like he was the all-knowing parent and she was just an ignorant kid. "I was just getting closure on something."

Gwen slumped her shoulders, lowered her voice in defeat. "Why did you need closure eight months later? You're with me now."

I felt my own shoulders deflate. *C'mon, Gwen.*

Andrew twisted his neck to crack it and then exhaled loudly, as if he was exasperated.

"Answer me," Gwen said, following him to the edge of the pool.

Andrew surveyed both the shallow and the deep end. The way he stood there recalled to my mind the way Dad stood one time, toothpick sticking out of his mouth, when Gram talked about seeing a dragonfly. Dad stood there until he couldn't take the discussion anymore—I knew us talking about signs used to drive him crazy—and left the room. I used to think he acted that way because it made him sad how Gram and I would keep Mom's spirit alive by talking about dragonfly visits and stuff during the summertime, but now I wasn't so sure.

"Why won't you answer me?" Gwen asked. She placed her hand on Andrew's arm, as if she were trying to empathize with the toxic situation that Andrew single-handedly started.

I witnessed Andrew's jaw clenching for just a moment before he began pacing back and forth like a caged animal. Then, he whipped around and shouted, "What do you want from me? I didn't even think we were serious the first few months! What, did you want to fight her or something?"

Gwen's ears grew red. She pushed aside an inflatable duck that had been tossed out of the deep end and stepped closer to Andrew in an attempt to talk out of everyone else's earshot. "Well, I thought we were serious. I wasn't going to *fight* her, I just didn't want her at my house. Why don't you understand that?"

Andrew laughed. "Stop being so intense, will you?" Then, erratically he pulled Gwen close and nudged her on the head like she was a little sister. "C'mon, lighten up, babe."

Gwen pulled away. "Stop it. This *is* serious in my opinion."

Andrew rubbed his brow like he was trying to erase a migraine. "Let's just talk about it later, all right?"

Gwen crossed her arms over her chest. "If you promise we will, then okay."

Then Andrew did this weird thing. He started to fake box, throwing small punches in front of his face while sneaking in taps on the side of Gwen's face.

"Stop," she said, turning her cheek.

"C'mon girl, ohhhh, watch out, she's got game," Andrew said, lightly smacking the side of her face again and then covering his face with his fists in feigned protection.

"Stop, Andrew," Gwen said, trying not to laugh, while his friends added fuel to the fire by laughing and teasing Gwen too. Andrew had this way, I realized, this charm and way of being funny in order to take the focus off his manipulative, messed-up behavior.

"C'mon now, girl, show me your game," Andrew said, shuffling his feet while he pretended to spar with Gwen.

"Cut it out. Seriously, you said we'd talk later but I don't see any better time really than right—"

In the matter of a second, I saw something cross Andrew's face. It was like he couldn't take another second of either Gwen complaining or of everyone looking to see what he'd say or do next in response. Suddenly he picked up Gwen off the concrete and threw her over his shoulder. Holding her mid-section while she shrieked, he jumped into the pool.

"What the hell was that?" Frankie blurted out.

Sputtering and coughing, Gwen swam to the surface, the sleeves of her white eyelet blouse ballooning above the water. Under the guise of being playful, his wet hair slicked back like a greaser, Andrew pushed her back under the water, while his friends laughed from the sidelines.

Gwen swam away and used the small ladder to climb out of the pool. She grabbed a towel and avoided everyone's stares as she looked down at the concrete.

With his biceps extra flexed, Andrew pushed himself up and out of the water. "C'mon babe," he laughed. "Lighten up."

Gwen fought back tears, her shirt and shorts drenched.

Frankie stepped closer to Andrew. "Dude, that wasn't cool."

Andrew's smile faded fast. From top to bottom, he scrutinized Frankie's scrawny frame. "What are you going to do about it?"

Gwen hurried over, her hair askew, her faded yellow beach towel hugging her shoulders. She stepped in between Frankie and Andrew and the Marshton guys who had strutted over, stubbing her toe on the concrete. "Stop, both of you."

I bit my lip, wanting to say something, but no words would come out. Instead, that other realm, *my other world,* continued to communicate with me, showing me an image behind my eyes, of a cloud bursting into smoke, and a man in a black cape, similar to a magician, who hid something under his cloak. The message: Andrew still had plenty up his sleeve.

I knew, in that instant, my dream hadn't yet materialized.

"Wait. Your friend gets in my face and you're telling me to stop?" Andrew said like Gwen was the one being irrational. "Well, maybe I better go too, then, just like Sophia did."

"No, that's not what I mean," Gwen said, tilting her head.

"No, no, I see how it is." Andrew held his hands up like he was under arrest. He stepped around the four-seated table covered with plates of half-eaten food by the grill. "You're choosing your Hanley friends over me. Let's go, everyone."

I pinched the inside of my arm, trying to hold back the feelings of wanting to punch Andrew in the face myself as his friends grabbed the last burgers off the grill. Meanwhile, Frankie and I were more than just Hanley friends.

"Don't go. I didn't choose anyone, I'm just saying . . ." Gwen said, trying to reason with Andrew, as if he might be a normal person with a normal brain.

"Dude, you embarrassed Gwen," Frankie interrupted.

Andrew trudged back over and stood toe-to-toe with Frankie. "Don't speak for my girlfriend," he said in a threatening tone.

"Leave it alone, Frankie, I'm fine," Gwen said, blinking back tears. I could barely look at her, my best friend's dignity evaporating before my eyes.

"You heard her, she's fine," Andrew said, thrusting out his chest. Looking down at Gwen, he said, "Why don't you tell your Hanley friends to go then, so we can talk in private?"

With red-rimmed eyes, Gwen looked at Frankie first and then at me. "Just go home, guys."

I clenched my fists, feeling as if the stone pavers were separating beneath my feet. "I think he's the one that needs to leave, Gwen."

Andrew scoffed. "You heard her—all the single ladies can go do something else." His loser friends laughed from behind the table.

"I don't believe I was talking to you," I said, straight to Andrew's hardened face. "I'm talking to my best friend."

A flash of anger shadowed Andrew's face so fast, I wasn't sure anyone else saw it but me. It was like a switch had been turned on inside him, though his eyes appeared cold.

Another knowing came to me, hitting me square in the chest, that Andrew lived for chaos, to fight, to have a reason to unleash some buried, inner rage.

"Gwen," I said, trying to get her attention, trying to act on the information I was being given from that other, faraway place.

"I think you should go," Gwen said as she stared at the ground. The summer breeze caused an empty bag of chips to roll past her feet. "I'm not going to make my boyfriend leave. Just let it go."

I felt like I was punched in the stomach. It was as if she had become a robot under the command of her owner. I stood there with my mouth open while Andrew dramatically nodded, ranting in the background about how she did the right thing.

"C'mon," Frankie said, taking my elbow to leave.

Burning inside myself, I started to follow Frankie out of the yard when Andrew made a disgusting sound and then spit loudly besides Frankie's foot, leaving a nasty mess on the pavers Gwen's dad, Doug, prided himself on keeping pristine.

"Low life," Frankie said under his breath.

Gwen tore off a paper towel from the holder and crouched down to clean up Andrew's mess, never looking at Frankie or me as we left the backyard—the yard we played in and swam in and coveted all our lives, practically considering it our own. That is, until Andrew appeared.

I left Frankie at the end of the driveway without a word, fighting back tears as I stomped along the path back toward my house. A heavy pressure built in my chest, and I knew Frankie felt the same way I did. There weren't any words to express the fact that I had officially just lost my best friend.

CHAPTER TWELVE

By the end of Thursday night's class, I hadn't had a hit in any of the exercises. Not even one speck of evidence that came close to meaning something and showcasing skill. Even Lisa did better than me, which made me feel like most of the class,—outside of Walter and Ed—were advancing. Maybe I simply had experienced a good case of beginner's luck.

To make matters worse, I couldn't recall half of what Allison taught during the entire two-and-a-half-hour class. It was like having chicken pox—no matter how many times I tried to let go of the thoughts about Gwen giving all her power away to her evil boyfriend, the urge to itch kept coming back.

"Hey there," Bobby said, coming over to me when the class ended, since he had sat in the front row. A newly sharpened pencil was tucked behind his ear. "We didn't hear from you tonight. Everything okay?"

I looked up at his genuinely concerned face, into those perfectly ocean blue eyes, growing painfully aware that my eyes probably looked like I was coming down with a spring flu or something, since they tended to gloss from burn when I was overly tired. "Yeah, I'm fine," I said. I wished I didn't always feel the need to say I was okay when I wasn't.

"All right, then," Bobby said, tapping the table with his pencil. Ed said good night to Bobby as he pushed in his chair, though he ignored me, even after three weeks of class. Maybe he thought I had some Gen Z disease. "I didn't know if your friend's situation was still bothering you, or maybe you had something else on your mind."

The whole thing felt so high school, when he asked me what might be wrong. I watched the adult men and women push in their chairs, toss water bottles in the trash, get on their cell phones, back to their mature lives. It wasn't immature high school drama, though. It was about knowing something and not being able to prove how I knew, and having to desperately wait for things to reveal themselves, desperately wanting them to— even if it meant that my best friend got hurt in the end.

They, Bobby included, didn't understand that I lived by my dreams—it wasn't just about my best friend or some typical girl drama that happened when you were a teenager—it was about my dreams being right about my best friend.

I also wanted to tell him that what else was on my mind was that I wanted to help people, to not make the same mistake I made with Denise, and that this was my chance to help Gwen, to figure out how to get her away from Andrew before he broke her heart. Even though part of me, in a way I'd never tell anyone else, wanted Gwen to hurt, to get her to see what had happened, what she had settled for, and who she had become.

But I didn't know Bobby well enough to say all this out loud, even though, for some weird reason, he made me feel really comfortable, considering he was the best-looking guy I knew.

I bit the side of my thumbnail, knowing right then and there who I might be able to talk to, who I might be able to ask for advice. I looked at Bobby. "I'm good, really. Thanks for checking in, though."

Once Bobby accepted my answer without pressuring me and left the room, I turned around to catch Gloria, who was gathering her large pocketbook and small Whole Foods insulated tote bag to leave. "Can I ask you something?"

Gloria checked her watch. "Of course, dear. Not too long, though, I'm meeting a friend and now that it's raining, I'm going to have to drive a little slower."

I continued to gain some nerve as the class dwindled down in size. "I . . . I wanted to ask you about my friend, the one you mentioned, to get your advice again, you know, on what I should do. She's not getting it, like at all, and I . . . ."

Gloria took off her red-rimmed reading glasses and placed them in her purse. "Devon, one of the hardest things in the world is realizing you can't help those who don't want to be helped."

I cracked my knuckles. "I know, but it's just that I'm sort of worried."

Gloria stared at me for a moment and then set both bags down on the table. She hesitated a moment and then closed her eyes.

I could hear Allison finishing up a conversation on the phone. Finally, I was about to get an answer, from a real-life medium, who could tell me once and for all what I needed to do to get my best friend back.

"Grandmother? Mother?" Gloria asked me with her eyes still closed.

Heat shot up through my body. "Huh? What do you mean?"

Gloria opened one eye. "Did you lose a grandmother?"

"Yes," I said, feeling as if my feet were now nailed to the ground. "Both my grandmother and my mother died."

Gloria closed her eyes again. "They're with you," she said. "Your mom, though. She wants you to know that she's with you. She feels very close, actually, something about a part of her being right there. That's the message coming to me." She smiled and opened her amber eyes, picking up her bags to go.

I pinched my hand. No offense to Gloria, but I already knew my mom was with me. Gram had taught me that. I needed to know something else about Gwen, about Andrew, about that party in the woods with the blond girl, or anything specific that meant my dreams were right.

Gloria checked her watch again, and I knew that was the end of that. Knowing she had taken the time, and that Allison probably needed to shut down the room, I simply said, "Thanks."

She squeezed my shoulder before she left. "Get some sleep, dear. You're exhausted."

I stared at the floor for a moment, fidgeting with my necklace. I slid my phone off the table and turned to leave, Allison and I the only two people left in the room. She looked up at me while she powered down her laptop. "Devon, can I speak with you for a moment?"

Blood rushed to my cheeks. "Sure," I shrugged. Did she hear what I had asked? Did she think I was pathetic for asking Gloria for help with my friend?

"I'm not sure what's going on in your life right now, but I want to offer you some valuable guidance, being that I've worked with police departments for over a decade. Are you ready to receive it?"

I nodded, feeling hollow inside my stomach—what it might feel like to be standing in the principal's office after getting in trouble.

"You're a young girl. This is hard work, professional work. You are dealing with professional people, most of them men, whether in this small-town department or in other departments, who deal with difficult themes, on a daily basis—things like burglaries, domestic violence, drug overdoses, especially drug overdoses as of late, abductions and killings. In some of these adults' opinions, and I'm still not certain where I fall on this spectrum, you still haven't finished developing psychologically at your age, and therefore may not be up for this type of work, even on a part-time, consultant-type basis. Now, having said that, I couldn't help but hear you were worried about something, which makes sense to me now that you never offered anything to be put on the board this evening. Are you feeling like you need some outside assistance?"

I shifted my stance. Had they considered me for consultant work? What did that even mean? Would it be called forensic psychic work like Gloria suggested? "What do you mean by outside assistance?"

Allison lowered her chin. "I'm quite sure the department could recommend a local counselor or psychological services, or even contact the guidance department at your high school, if you are in need of speaking with someone about something that's troubling you."

My entire face was on fire. Why did it always come back to counseling? Was Allison going to tell Len I wasn't on pace with everyone else, with one week left of class to prove myself? Is that where she was going to land on "the spectrum?" That perspective would kill my chances of being asked to stay on for the advanced session. "No, that won't be necessary," I said, in an attempt to sound older and more confident than I felt in that moment.

Did Allison even have a clue of what my dreams showed me night after night? Of girls being attacked, and missing kids in basements? Did this stuff ever happen to her? Or was she some criminal justice major who found herself in this teaching position because of some theory? Did she know my mother killed herself before I even had the chance to really know her? Did she think I had come to this remote viewing workshop by chance or that it was fun for me?

"You're sure?" Allison said. She stared at me in that way that made me feel she was sizing me up again, as if I needed help, the same way my father had made me feel like I needed help when I told him I saw my mother standing in my room the night he took me to the hospital.

"Yes, I'm sure," I said, trying to keep my voice from cracking.

Despite the fact that I had nothing to show in tonight's class that proved I had a talent worth working with, and what felt like yet another epic failure, there was no way I was going to end the class by failing and have Dad say, "I told you so."

"Well, then, I'll take your word for it," Allison said, zipping up her laptop case.

Her husband left her, cheated on her with one of her friends. The words floated into my mind while I listened to her speak. I understood right then what made Allison so tightly wound. "However, you've got to learn how to keep whatever is going on in your life in check. If you want to do this work, you have to leave your worries at the door."

I don't know how part of me could have felt bad for Allison as I left the conference room, but I did—that I knew this about her, that she *was more focused on work than anything else in her life* and that's what made her husband cheat. The thing was, I didn't need, or care, to be right about information on my intimidating, all-work-and-no-play, remote-viewing instructor.

I needed to be right about Andrew and, more importantly, for Gwen to see how the information from my dreams would help her get away.

CHAPTER THIRTEEN

I arrived home to an empty house. Not just empty, but entirely unlit. The Uber driver left me standing in the dark as he backed out of my driveway. It wasn't as if I didn't know Dad had gone to some country concert tonight with Tina, since he instructed me, via text during my break, to take an Uber home from class and not to panic about it. It's just that I didn't know until I got the Post-It memo, along with thirty dollars to order Mamma Mia's since "we hadn't been there in a while," that he planned to stay the night at Tina's place afterward, and that he'd see me tomorrow night after he got off work.

I yanked open the refrigerator to grab a class of orange juice, cursing my father out loud. I knew having Dad home wouldn't have made a difference in the way I felt about what

Allison said, or about how I didn't do well in the class tonight and may have blown my chances to get a spot in the advanced class or a potential career for that matter, or about Gwen and her ridiculously dysfunctional relationship. It just would have been nice to have my father home, a parent home, *someone* to take my pulse to see if I was okay today, or okay with life in general, for God's sake.

But PJ Alante didn't think that way. And probably never would.

I gulped down the juice, liquid spilling down the side of my face. My father thought mostly about himself and the fun he planned to have when he wasn't working. It was on nights like these, when I needed my father most, when I needed a parent of some kind, that I realized Dad was never really there physically anymore, never mind the emotional way I always wanted and needed him to be.

As much as I would have liked Mamma Mia's at that moment, I considered that if I did order a pizza, it was like my father would have won. I made myself a sandwich with the rest of the turkey Avo had brought over earlier in the week, on the last two slices of stale bread, stuffing it into my mouth as I choked back tears. I ruminated over all the times I could recall that my father hadn't shown up in my life. It was well after midnight once I finally retreated to my room, shaky and unable to calm down.

I paced the floor, waiting for the melatonin I had taken to kick in and help me sleep, knowing full well it might be another rough night. I desperately wanted to pick at my skin but tried hard not to. I knew Dad would just start a fight with me over that if he saw the marks again, hopefully not taking me back to the hospital like he did last time, missing the point of why I picked my skin altogether.

I pinched my lip as I stepped back and forth across the carpet, giving me something to grab onto as I thought back to Gloria and what she said about my mother. Maybe Gloria wasn't that great of a medium after all. Even though she did get that I lost my grandmother and mother, and when she was in a hurry. She still could have been grasping at straws, though, since a lot of kids my age didn't have their grandparents. I dug my fingernail into the sensitive skin in my bottom lip. Not their mothers, though.

She feels very close, I heard Gloria say inside my mind, *part of her is right there.*

I kicked at the pile of laundry on my floor. *Duh. Random advice.* What else would a medium say to a girl who had lost her mother?

The wind picked up outside, bringing a sudden gust in through my opened window. I heard one of Old Man Coleman's stray cats let out a shrill scream. Shuddering, I stepped across the room to shut the window beside my bed, suddenly remembering the information a lady had given me at the psychic fair last year about praying to Archangel Michael.

I pulled open my side table drawer and grabbed my journal, feverishly flipping through the written pages. Drawing my finger along the lines, I held my breath until I located the message.

My eyes darted across the page before I raised them a few inches above my journal, lost in thought. Gram had encouraged me to write down my feelings in my journals, to *write the story of my life,* and *all my feelings, when no one else seemed to understand.*

I suddenly wondered—and felt surprised that I never thought of this before—whether my mother had kept a journal. If she had been able to tell the story of her life, and write down all her feelings, would things have ended differently?

The weight of what could have been hit me hard in the chest, threatening to knock the wind out of me. Already curled over, I crouched down beside my bed to pray.

Clasping my hands against my forehead, like after receiving communion at church on holidays, I whispered in the dark, "Archangel Michael, I forgot about you and what that angel card reader told me about praying to you last year. I'm sorry for that. I've always prayed to Gram when I've needed something, but maybe I'm supposed to pray to you when I need something really big to happen. Like right now. The way I feel trying to get rid of these obsessive thoughts that obviously I can't do anything about and that are interfering with me moving forward in my life. I want to make something of myself, to do something special, something helpful.

"That sword the lady last year said you gave to me, the sword you give to seekers of the truth, so they can become warriors, too? Well, I'm trying to use it. I'm trying to be a warrior and to fiercely protect my gifts like you said. But the dreams haven't proved true. And I still can't let them go. They keep coming into my head. It's driving me crazy! I don't want to think about Andrew, or even Gwen anymore! I just want to work on cases with the police, even if they're not exactly real cases yet and only class exercises. I know I need to start somewhere. I just need to be given a chance. If you hear me, and if you forgive me for not praying to you sooner, I need you to help me, Archangel Michael, to prove to the Hanley

Police Department that I deserve to be in that advanced class. That I can be a forensic psychic detective and help people."

I squeezed my hands hard, choking back tears when I thought of the idea of not being asked to be included over the summer session. If Len, or the others, thought I might be too young, too immature—unable to *get myself in check,* like Allison had warned me before I left class tonight. "In the name of justice, though, the way you told me to do this work, I'd kind of like to be right, not in a hey-everybody-look-at-me kind of way, but to be right about Andrew, so that he gets what he deserves and I can move on with my life. To be clear, I'd really like to be asked to stay on for the second remote viewing session at the department. That would mean a lot to me. It would make me feel like I had some kind of future."

My hands trembled and I felt a wavering in my throat. "I've done what the dreams asked me to do; I spoke up, I told my best friend about her boyfriend cheating on her in the dream. It's not helping. Nothing is helping, and now I'm not doing well at the station. They probably think I had some kind of beginner's luck, and they're ready to laugh me right back to high school, where they think I belong. But I don't belong there. I want more for myself, to make something of my life. College isn't for me and I don't want to work for my father."

Suddenly, a coiling energy rose up from the base of my spine, my body shaking as if an earthquake started moving the metaphoric tectonic plates inside of me. A flash of a wall I hadn't known existed began crumbling down inside my chest, privy only to my clairvoyant mind.

Uncontrollably, I began to sob. "Whatever, or whoever, sends me these dreams in the first place, you need to help me. Show me that my dreams mean something, that they're here to help people, that I'm right. Please. Archangel Michael, Gram, Mom, whoever it is who maybe wants me to use them to do good, please hear me."

CHAPTER FOURTEEN

The next morning, I woke to pans clanking in the kitchen. I winced, knowing Avo was here for her usual Friday visit, making something for dinner so we'd also have leftovers for the weekend— something she often did when I was at school. I pulled the covers tighter over my head, trying to remember my dreams.

Shit. *School.*

What time was it, anyway? Did I even have a dream? I couldn't recall a thing.

I pulled the covers over my face. Then I heard my heavy-footed grandmother making her way down the hall toward my bedroom.

My heart raced, that first symptom of anxiety I knew so annoyingly well.

I cursed Avo under the covers for waking me with all her clanking, blaming her for the fact that I had been interrupted from my dream state.

"Devon, are you awake?"

I closed my eyes tight. Why hadn't I dreamed? I prayed hard, but I got nothing. Plus, I still felt exhausted. What kind of answer to my prayer was that?

"Good morning, gorgeous," Avo said, sliding the covers off my face to give me a kiss like she did when I was little, when I appreciated those kinds of loving gestures. I rolled onto my side, yanking the covers back over my head. "Your father said you've been tired and grumpy this week, so I wanted to let you sleep, but it's 9:30 now, and time to get up for the day. Come sit with me while I finish the sausage and pork lasagna you love. I'll write you a sick note later."

I grumbled under my breath. *Funny. Dad acknowledges I'm tired, but doesn't bother to ask why and neither does my grandmother. Yet, she'll write a note for me, no problem.* I kicked at the covers. *My family sucks.*

"Come now, you can rest while I finish cooking," Avo said. She tidied the blankets after I kicked them to the bottom of the bed.

I begrudgingly followed Avo down the matted hall carpet, trying to recall any fragment of a dream. Rain hit the roof while I stared at my grandmother's open-footed Rockport sandals—the ones that prompted Dad and Uncle Rob to call her Jesus whenever she wore them. Why didn't I get one message, one piece of information that told me someone on the other side was listening? Maybe I should have prayed straight to Jesus.

"Don't worry, your father will be home for supper tonight, in case that's what's causing your attitude," Avo said, in her gruff but well-meaning tone as she ladled the final layer of sauce atop the lasagna noodles.

"I don't have an attitude," I said, stepping past the hutch beside the basement door and across from the kitchen table. I stared through the glass sliders, checking for a sign from the birds, to see if any were perched at the feeder. Nope. Not even a sparrow.

"Respect your father," Avo said. She sprinkled Romano cheese on top of the sauce before sliding the glass pan in the oven.

"What do you mean?"

"Try not to bring up these detective classes of yours at the dinner table," she said. She wiped her hands on the dishtowel before folding the sauce-stained cloth into a neatened square. "Men don't like a lot of talk after a hard day's work."

I glanced over at my stocky, five-foot-tall grandmother, the old beige apron she always brought with her hanging loosely from the back of her thick neck. I wanted to ask her if she was living in the 1950s, but instead, raising my brow, said, "I'm surprised you even knew about the class."

She folded the dishrag into an even smaller square, the stains nonexistent from view. "Your father tells me what he needs to. And what you need to hear from me is this: I don't want you stressing your father with what you're learning or doing in that class of yours, or whatever is causing you to not sleep again. Your father's been through enough. The both of you have."

I took a swig of the juice Avo had set out for me on the island counter. "I'm not trying to stress him out. I'm trying to figure something out. It'd be nice for a change if someone asked me how I'm doing, instead of just offering to write me a note for school."

Avo kept her head down while she washed the remaining dishes in the sink. "Your family knows you better than anyone. Remember that. I watched your mother struggle, Devon Elise, and I didn't say anything, because she had her own mother, but you're my granddaughter and I'm not having any of this stress you're putting on yourself, walking around tired all the time, no matter what you might have inherited from your mother."

I pressed my thumb hard against the design in the juice glass. Could Avo tell me something about my mother that might help me? "Why was she anxious?" I asked. I cleared my throat. "Was it because she had me so young?"

"Nonsense," Avo said, waving her hand. "We all raise babies and do just fine. Even when we're young, even when it's hard. I suppose your mom had mental illness in her genes, that's all. But there's no sense talking about it now. Just keep it nice for your father when he gets home is what I'm telling you. Now, do you want a cup of tea?"

The rain descended on the roof like darts. Mental illness? Gram never told me my mother had mental illness or that it might have run in the family. Gram didn't seem like she had anything wrong with her, except maybe being too nice at times when my dad didn't agree with her about all the signs—birds, dragonflies, heart rocks—she said showed up from my mom in heaven.

Gram never even defended herself when my father scoffed or chuckled, like it was all made up and imaginary. She just shrugged and said okay, like he was the one in charge, which I guess he was since he was my father, but still.

The more I thought about it, I remembered how Gram could be a little neurotic about cleaning. She was always cleaning the counters, the walls, the floors, but I always thought she just kept a clean house for me because I went there so often. I remembered now that Avo said once that people cleaned like that when they couldn't control things that happened in life.

Did intensely cleaning constitute mental illness, though? Like some kind of OCD? Maybe my grandfather had mental illness? I never really knew him since he died when I was a baby, but no one ever mentioned anything about him being mentally ill. Is this what Gram wanted me to know? Did I have a dream about it last night or was this the message I needed to hear, after all this time?

While Avo put away the clean pots and pans, a gray, hole-like shape formed in my mind. The shape, it's form—a black hole? Hard to decipher. I felt like the message might be more about what Avo told herself—that using a term like mentally ill as a way of explaining why my mother had taken her life made Avo feel better about the whole thing.

I gripped the juice glass with both hands. Who cared enough to make me feel better about my stuff? Not Gram, my mom, or even Archangel Michael himself had bothered to send me any kind of message to make me feel better about my life at the moment.

"Well, everything's cleaned up," Avo said. She quickly glanced over at the hutch before checking the time on the microwave. "I have to go meet Eleanor for coffee up at Crossroads, so I'll need you to take that out of the oven when the timer beeps. Don't get distracted on your phone. Enjoy your dinner with your father later. A nice lasagna is what the two of you need."

I didn't look my grandmother in the eye when she picked up her purse from the kitchen table, still feeling sore she woke me from my dreams, potentially causing me to miss an opportunity I so desperately needed.

"Remember, your family always knows what you need," Avo said, giving me a kiss on the cheek.

I watched my grandmother waddle down the hall and close the door behind her, silently screaming inside myself that I didn't want any of her stupid lasagna.

Everyone thought they knew. But no one knew what I needed.

Brooding, I noticed the bottom drawer of the hutch. Avo had apparently forgot to close it. I tried to kick it shut with my foot from where I was sitting, but it was so stuffed with all the paperwork my father kept crammed in there, it wouldn't close.

Frustrated, I crouched down to throw away some of the take-out menus, business cards, and clutter when I heard the familiar chirp of the cardinal at the feeder.

My heart pulsed against my chest, hearing that familiar sound of hope at the spiritual sign for my maternal grandmother.

Slowly at first, the chirps grew louder. I turned toward the sliders. *Gram. Do you have something to tell me? I'm listening. I'm sorry I got mad that you didn't send me a dream.*

The red bird pecked away at the recently filled feeder, like it had found some kind of secret treasure. *Please, Gram. Help me.*

The bird continued chirping, frantically now, it seemed to me, yet no flashes or words appeared in my mind.

All feelings of hope lost, I turned back to the hutch and pulled the drawer off the runner, dumping its contents all over the floor.

That's when I noticed the familiar frail handwriting written across a musty, business-sized manila envelope.

Outside, the cardinal continued to chirp.

Written in blue ink across the package: *Kathleen's Journal, I.*

CHAPTER FIFTEEN

I holed myself up in my room. The grassy, beige canvas journal with the cracked binding felt dusty and dry, yet *gentle* and *kind* in a way I couldn't explain, as strange as that sounds, in my shaking hands. I sat there for a few minutes just holding it. Lyrics from that old Kenny Rogers' song *Lady* floated through my mind for some reason as I touched the rough ridges in the cloth cover. In the deepest part of my heart, I knew that once I opened this book, my life would change. For better or worse, I didn't yet know.

I didn't know anything, except the fact that I had my mother's thoughts, feelings, possible dreams about her future, and maybe even the answers to why she did what she did, right here in my hands.

I opened the book. The first entry was dated January 14, the day after my mother's birthday. I thought for a moment, glancing over at a stitched square in my comforter. She would have been twenty-three. With no inscription on the inside cover, there was no indication the journal had been a gift from someone else, like Gram had written on the inside page when she gave my journal to me.

It made me wonder if my mother had gone to an actual store, in search of something to write down all she was feeling. I stared out my window. The upper branches of the tall oaks that stood at the end of our property swayed in the wind and rain. Maybe she had ordered the originally pretty journal online, in secret—I think online was available then—waiting for the package to arrive so my dad wouldn't know. The same way I kept mine hidden in my drawer so he didn't find out how I really felt most of the time.

I turned back to the daintily written words on yellowed pages. She had filled every crevice of every corner with her words. If mom was twenty-three, that means I had turned four in December—only a year and a half before she took her life, her shortened life, before everything changed, the missed opportunity of what might have been.

He's out again. But I guess that's why I bought this journal in the first place. I need someone or something to trust, to talk about it all. About him. My heart hurts so badly inside my chest, I feel like I'm going to have a heart attack. I can't even put nail polish on to look somewhat pretty cause my nails are bitten down to the skin. I feel gross. I stare in the mirror and find every flaw about myself—my light skin, the nicks in my face after I pick at it, my flat hair, my stomach that used to be flat. I feel so ugly all the time. I know he's probably out flirting, drinking with his friends at the bars. Did I really expect anything different? Did he ever think I might want to go, too—to the places we used to go together with our fake IDs— and have fun? But if I'm being honest, and that's also the reason I bought this journal: to be honest with at least something that cared to listen to what I had to say, really say, all the things I've been screaming inside myself to say. Then, the truth is, I'd actually rather be home watching movies, working on being a family, watching TV like other couples do, after Devon goes to sleep. I never really wanted to be one of the townies who goes to the local bars all the time, even though Dad, in a moment of frustration I'm sure, said that's how he saw my future. I just kind of thought, at this point, that the three of us would be a little family—isn't that what we're supposed to be doing, working on being a family now that we have a daughter? Or can we really call ourselves a family? The other truth is, though it hurts me to see the words on paper: PJ and I are two teenagers who had a baby, caught up in the passion of being in love, kids ourselves, too stupid to think we needed protection. I'm so stupid sometimes!! Two teenagers, who, if they didn't have a baby, might have gone to college—at least I would have—and now be working and living life like everyone else our age is doing. Which is what PJ is doing—the working part and having fun—but I'm not. Not the college part, the working part, and having a little fun. I still love PJ so much—he's my first real love!—but he's different now, or maybe he's the same and it's me who's different? We're not kids anymore. We had to grow up fast. I hate that part. I hate myself for being so dumb . . . I just feel so alone. Does he even love me anymore? He barely looks me in the eye when I ask him if he still wants to be with me. Did he just love me before, when things were easier and carefree and I looked prettier, like when he first met me and I was popular and cute? I wasn't the prettiest girl in school, but he used to tell me I was. He seemed so obsessed with me all the time, it made me feel like I was a princess. I just thought you were supposed to automatically love someone more after you had a baby. I keep asking myself if I did something wrong. Maybe I do need to act more carefree and more relaxed, and not make him mad the way I always seem to. I wish he'd just tell me what I can do to make things better between us. I asked him again last night but he just blows it off, like I'm being crazy for thinking stuff like that, but I think he just can't deal with feelings, hard feelings. All I do is think about things. Like how to look prettier, how to act more cool to please him. I can't stop thinking. What else is there to do besides taking care of our daughter? I feel guilty for even writing that down.

I feel like such a bad person when I think things like that. It's just that I can't stop thinking how hard it is to be a mother, never mind one who still feels like a kid herself. It's so unfair when PJ leaves. There's nothing I can do about it! Like go and make HIM jealous or anything, the way I used to when he'd do that to me, making me jealous when he'd talk to other girls in school and at parties. I feel so trapped! (Okay, I'm back . . . I just stopped writing to pick at my face until it bled and now I feel even worse about myself!!!) I just wonder if we even would have stayed together after high school, even though we always swore we would. Maybe I really am just stupid about life, like common-sense wise—and dreaming about wanting to make it as a real family. Well, I know I'm a dreamer—in terms of having actual dreams anyway—and no one can take that from me, at least.

I sat up on my knees and turned the page.

February 1. I do love being a mother. I really do. I can't just go out whenever I want to, like I used to. Mom told me it would be like this. Not that she wanted me to do anything different about my situation—she and Dad wanted me to get married and "do the right thing," even though Dad couldn't look at me, I swear to God, for months.

Mom warned me it would be hard. They don't even know about the pushing or the shoving—they just think we fight all the time like we used to in high school about stupid stuff—they don't know how he grabs my arm, hard, and worse, whenever I yell at him, or get in his face about where he goes at night after he comes home buzzed. Isn't that my right???? Plus, when I had that dream that he was out with someone else, I felt like it really happened, or that it will, and then I feel like I can't breathe. I haven't said anything to him about the dream, though. I know he'd get mad, probably make fun of me and

call it "just another stupid dream." Mom
even said, "They're just dreams" when I
told her about that one. Which took a
lot for me to do . . . .

It took me a minute to notice that I dug into my arm so hard
I broke the skin in another section. *She picked at her face, her skin.
She did the same stuff I did.* Except that she was so hard on herself.
My mother was so hard on herself. I stared at the marks I made on
my arms. I hadn't done that in so long—at least not make a mark,
anyway. I clenched my hands together and squeezed hard so I
wouldn't do further damage. For myself, but for her, too, in some
weird way that wasn't going to change a thing.

Then there was the other piece. Did my mother dream the
same way I did? Or was it just the regular kind of dreams people
had once in a while that really freaked them out? They seemed so
much like mine though, the part about wondering if something
had yet to happen. Never mind the fact that I felt like I was spying
on my father, knowing things about him that my mother wrote
in secret that weren't for me to know, yet I basically knew anyway.

He was the same way now.

He never liked to talk about things, especially the hard
things. He stayed out late.

He thought I was crazy, too, had taken me to the
hospital for it.

But the pushing and the shoving, I had only seen him do
that to other people. People who messed with him—over work
or his character or whatever people fight about when they're
flirting with other guys' girlfriends in bars. Dad was known as a

"hothead," especially to people who weren't in his family. I just hadn't known he was a hothead to my mother.

I caught the tail end of a yellow finch fly past my window. I guess I *was* spying on my dad in a way, and on Gram too, since I hadn't realized she had dealt with my mother in that dismissive way—such a different way than she spoke to and treated me. But even though technically I might be spying on two people I loved, I also knew for a fact that journal wasn't in the bottom kitchen drawer before—Avo had to have put it there for me to find. Which made it okay that technically I might have been spying, at least in my eyes.

April 16. Am I a nag? I try to let PJ feel like he's free to go and have fun after working all day, even though it makes me want to crawl out of my skin. Plus, I can't sleep. It's not that I don't appreciate his working hard, or his family letting us live here, with every piece of furniture from them, and how they buy us groceries and everything. I do! My family can't help us, although they try. They're just barely getting by. I hate when PJ says I'm not appreciative—honestly I am!—or when he says all I focus on is what's wrong. I'm just tired all the time and feel like crying every single day and now I'm on

this birth control pill and I don't know
if it's that, even though everyone says
it's not and that I have to use it so I
don't get into a worse situation than I
already am. I feel like it might be this
medication adding to the way I feel.
Especially when I've been thinking this and
then the dragonflies appear. I feel like it's
a sign. They just show up right when
I'm thinking that medication is causing
my symptoms. But no one will listen to
me. I don't ever remember hating myself
so much, either, or not liking the way
I look or I feel, though the doctor said
it takes a while for hormones to calm
down. But Devon is four now! Is it
because I'm young? I wonder what kind
of a job I would have had if I made
it to college. Maybe PJ's right—stop
thinking so much and get my head out
of the clouds and "just chill." Maybe I
wouldn't have done anything and just
had some job in town, a good-paying
job that helped with the bills. But then
that makes me feel guilty, too, how I
don't help with money. Even when he

gets physical with me, and I know that part's not okay and everything, but it's what he says. It's like it overshadows his other bad behavior and gets in my head, how I'm not able to help pay bills and do my part financially. Then I end up feeling like a bad person and I can't stop thinking like that. It makes me feel worthless.

I pressed my hand over my necklace and into my chest, hoping it would brand a mark into my skin. *Dragonflies.* That's where Gram got the sign. Which means she knew about the journal, too. A journal that, page after delicate page, was filled with guilty, exhausted, ruminating, unexpressed-to-anyone-else feelings. Having read three-quarters of the way through, I couldn't help but think that my mom felt like she might break in half, as if my mother was a fragile angel figurine sitting high up on a shelf that you needed to be extra careful with when you dusted.

I glanced at my bureau, Dad's old bureau from when he grew up. Then I looked around my room at the bed, the night table, the laundry bin, the old curtains that had gathered dust now that Avo didn't clean them the way she used to at the beginning of every spring. I imagined myself as my mom, if she were sitting here, and how she must have felt so alone.

I turned the book over and set it down on my comforter, right before I dug my nail into my skin purposely trying to make it bleed, not caring about anything except wanting to tell my mother it would have been okay, that she shouldn't have felt bad, especially settling for someone who put their hands on her in not a nice way.

I wanted to tell her that of course she was tired; from having me, from having a baby so young, and missing out on what her friends were doing, from not going to college and realizing her dreams, from not having a husband who offered her any emotional support or had class enough to keep his oversized hands to himself. Also, that I believed in the signs. I believed in the dragonflies.

Inhaling sharply, tears flooding my eyes, a sudden ascent of energy rose in my throat that I didn't feel coming. The colors red and gray flooded every inch of my clairvoyant mind like a house fire that couldn't be controlled. The image, the feelings, *anger toward my father*—no *rage*—filled every cell in my body with metaphorical flames and smoke. How he didn't know what my mom was feeling. How he continually minimized her concerns, her exhaustion, *the signs she saw as hope.* He only focused, in classic fashion, on himself and his work, and of course, having fun—and it sounded like with more than a few women. Or maybe he didn't know how Mom felt because she was too scared to tell him. Maybe he didn't care.

What did he expect my mother to do? Be happy in her lonely life with him?

I fought back the tears, the sudden urge to get on Janice's bike and ride to Alante's right now, in the middle of the day, and throw the journal at my father's feet, in front of Uncle Rob and his employees and his customers, committing the cardinal sin of discussing personal issues at work. I wanted so badly to embarrass him the way he had embarrassed my mother by getting physical with her, by being with other women in town. I knew about the possible cheating through random gossip, but now, reading it in first person, in viewing things from my mom's eyes, this apparent fact made me more angry—even though I'd read he did those things a long time ago. I thought it was because now it felt like I knew her. I was getting to know her better, and through that experience, getting to know my father a lot better, too.

Then I thought maybe I should wait until supper, knowing he was coming home tonight, for a change. Maybe I'd lay the journal out on the table by his glass of soda, beside his silverware, showing him that I knew, that I knew more than he already thought I knew, about the cheating—which to this day he never admitted or discussed with me, not that he would—and about my mom's depression, which to me seemed more like it was caused by my father's lame behavior than some "mental illness."

I took a deep breath, trying to think of the best thing to do, the right way to handle it, wondering if Dad even knew Mom had a journal all this time. Had Avo put it there for only me to find? Why was I just finding out about it now—did she think I couldn't handle it earlier in my life?

I slid my finger between the last few pages and the back cover of the book, not wanting it to end. I wanted to learn more about my mother, wishing she was here with me now to talk about things, like some mothers would, pulling out old journals and explaining to their daughters how they had felt when they wrote back then, and how they might feel differently now that they were older.

A pain seared in my side, like the gash of a sword, knowing she didn't have that chance. I wondered if I should continue reading or put the journal away and finish it later to make it last. I held the side of the worn canvas and closed my eyes, trying to focus on what to do.

An image of Gwen's face appeared. I tried to push it out of my mind, like *no, not now,* but then a thought struck me like a match—that how Gwen behaved seemed a lot like my mother, meaning the way my mom came across, doubting herself in the relationship, trying to please her man, like she was the one doing something wrong.

I opened my eyes and continued to read.

June 17. Am I crazy? I can't stop thinking about bad things. Never mind what I see in my dreams. No one gets it, or maybe they just don't want to understand. Not even my own mother. She keeps saying I "just need sleep," and maybe I do, but it's more than that. Why are they telling me to stay with him when they know how he is? He fights everyone in town! He used to fight over me . . . . Didn't they think the way he fights with other people might be happening to me in secret? Are people stupid? No, that's right, I'm the stupid one for staying. I feel like people in town look at me like I'm a fool, but I don't know if that's me just being paranoid? I feel like I have no one to talk to, no one who gets it, gets me, or wants to get me. And that makes me feel worse. And alone. Even though I have Devon, and I know I'm not alone, and despite all the hard feelings, she's the cutest little thing, a complete mix of PJ and me, with her light eyes like mine and her tanned skin like PJ's and a mix of our hair, this really pretty caramel kind of light brown—the kind I would have died to have. I really love her to pieces.

I thought it might hold out until the end. Instead, the dam burst inside me with two pages left to go. I leaned over my legs, tears dripping onto my knees.

She loved me to pieces.

Even though she was exhausted and felt alone, and missed out on her opportunity to go to college and be a regular kid her age, and no one understood her, *my mother loved me to pieces.*

I choked on my sobs, experiencing both happiness and sadness at the same time. A torrent of emotions swirled inside of me.

The sheer curtain swayed in the breeze beside the stocky, dark brown bureau. The bureau I never bothered to think about, how much it didn't fit me, how much I never cared to ask for a different, more feminine one.

I turned away to gather my thoughts. Did Dad love me to pieces? Did he even really love my mom or was it just some high school infatuation like Gwen had with Andrew? Or maybe my dad loved my mother in the only way he knew how and that was just his DNA—to work hard and then feel it was his right to go out every night and have his fun at the expense of others in his family. The exact same way he did things now, in his life with just me.

Except, he got physical with my mother.

I remembered hearing once that my grandfather was that way with Avo.

How Mom seemed similar to Gwen made me wonder if most guys acted that way at some point, after the relationship got serious.

I sunk down lower on my calves. Maybe I'd be like my mom, and Gwen, and feel the same way they did. How would I know, since I had never even been in a relationship? It's not like I had a lot of role models to follow—both my grandfathers passed before I was born and Frankie's parents split up when he was in first grade. Gwen's parents were still together, though, and they seemed okay, normal, I guess.

A thought drifted past my mind: maybe it depended on the guy, that the type of guy Dad was to my mom, and the type of guy Andrew is to Gwen, was the real problem. Maybe that's why the dream showed me both Andrew and Dad that first time, superimposed on top of each other. Maybe only *those kinds of guys* cheated, causing you to question yourself.

I stared at my closed bedroom door, chewing on my thumb, hoping I wouldn't ever settle for a relationship like theirs, when a puffy white cloud appeared in my mind. All billowy and pillow-like, the clouds began covering my worried thoughts, their message to ease my mind. It was as if someone wrapped me in a blanket in that moment, comforting me, whispering, *don't worry, you won't have a relationship like that,* almost telling me things I needed to know about my future.

A kindergarten bus chugged past in the downpour, making its way to the next stop on the street, toward the moms who waited in their raincoats to greet their children coming home from school. Moms who waited to hug their children with open arms.

She loved me to pieces.

My heart opened like angel wings and then immediately retreated, a closed fist inside my chest. Why, then, would my mother do what she did: take her own life, a year and a half later? Even though she said the birth control stuff might have made her feel worse, it didn't seem like she was high or drunk while she was writing, the way I had always been told things went down. I think I would have noticed in her writing if she had been intoxicated. I mean, I guess I might not be able to tell, but I kind of think I would. I made a mental note to never take birth control, even though I didn't need to worry about that at the moment, or ever.

I glanced down at the final two pages held between my fingers and then looked over at a spot on my bed. When *did* my mother start drinking and taking pills?

I took a deep breath and opened the rest of the journal.

June 23, He said he'd never cheat on me, but now I know he did for sure. I can't sleep. Or eat. It's been days. I also know he's lying about that girl he was with in the car—saying he was just driving her home cause her boyfriend left her at the bar. Like I'm stupid. Like I'm simple Hanley stupid, as if I would never have gotten out of this small town and went to college and had a life other than this one. I have to keep this journal hidden, but then again, he's not home enough to see me writing in it anyway. PJ's mother Ines, or Avo as Devon calls her, blew the whole thing off as usual, said he's just "passing fancy." I love Ines, but she NEVER goes against him, no matter what he does! As if I should just settle for someone who does that to me, like I'm not good enough for more. Am I? Maybe this is all there is. Even mom tells me I got myself into this mess, that this is my life now and I need to accept it, and that at least I have Devon. I wish I had ripped that girl out of the car, though, the way I wanted to when I drove looking for him and found him in the woods. He broke my heart. He broke my heart for good this time. I feel so alone.

My heart jammed in my throat.

My dream.

About the car—Dad with that woman. So *I had* seen him cheating. But what did that mean about Andrew?

I snapped the book shut and grabbed my own journal out of the drawer. I flipped the pages until I found the entry, how Dad and Andrew had appeared to be almost the same person. But what did that mean? Was the dream I had more about my father or Andrew? Had I made a mistake? Not to mention sitting here with the information that my father seemed like an abuser. Not *seemed*. It was there, in black and white, written on these pages. At times, he was an abuser.

The wall creaked and I looked up, second-guessing myself as I teetered between the dream being only about Dad or the idea that Andrew might still be a cheater too. Though I didn't have proof, yet. Was the creak a sign about Dad or Andrew?

A chill caused me to shudder. No. I clenched a section of my sheets. I knew I hadn't made a mistake. Andrew had to be a cheater, I was sure of it. What I wasn't sure of was whether my mom wrote solely for herself or if she wanted me, too, to know more about my father, through these journals. I already knew my dad cheated on my mother. Maybe she wanted me to know more about his behavior for a reason? Or was there something else?

The journal pages stirred from the wind whipping through my window. I felt an intense sense of stillness, of presence. I closed my eyes. What if the dream *was* about Andrew, but *brought by my mother*, to help me understand how Gwen felt? What if she gave me the dream to warn Gwen, so Gwen didn't make the same mistakes that *she* did?

My head pounded, as if I had just taken a final exam, trying to wrap my brain around the idea. I squinted. Was that even possible? For my mother to do something like that, from the other side?

I stared up through the palladium window, at a sliver of white clouds forming through the gray. If that *was* the case—if my idea was right, and my mother *had* sent me the dream, to help me in some way, to help Gwen—then my mother would also show me what I needed to do next.

CHAPTER SIXTEEN

When he arrived home from work later that Friday evening, my father whistled as he entered the kitchen.

I carefully placed the reheated tray of lasagna on the counter, my blood boiling.

He tossed his keys in the clay holder I had made for him in second grade and I knew, as I set the table for the two of us, that he had no idea Avo had put my mother's journal in the bottom of the hutch for me to find.

Avo had to have brought my mother's journal from her house and was the only one who knew it existed, other than, it seemed, Gram. It would be totally Avo's style to place it deep in the drawer for me to find on my own—otherwise, like if she had chosen to hand it to me, we would have had to have a conversation about the contents.

Staring at a spot on the wall beside the oak hutch and the basement door, I suddenly wondered if there was a second notebook, since the title read *Kathleen's Journal:1.*

"Avo wrote you a note for school when you go back Monday, right?" Dad asked, pulling up a seat at the table.

"Yup," I said.

"As long as you're keeping your grades up, they won't say nothing. They never said nothing to me in high school, and I wasn't half as smart as you." Dad moved his black, World's Best Dad mug out of the way, and shook open the Hanley paper. "You are keeping your grades up, right?"

"Yup," I said. I stared at my father while I ate my lasagna. Slowly, deliciously, I moved the food around my mouth, my heart beating fast in my chest while I watched him read the sports section. Checking on the baseball stats of the kids in town, no doubt, checking to see if anyone had ever surpassed his home run stats, the ones I had heard about for years at every Fourth of July cookout my family ever had.

Dad glanced up at me, but it occurred so fast I almost questioned if it happened at all. I played in my imagination for a moment. For a second, did my father wonder whether I was on to him as a person—what he did to my mom, what I now knew she felt about their relationship? I slid my feet under my chair, pressed my toes into the floor, waiting for the perfect time to say something, even though I still didn't know what.

Dad continued to check his phone between drinking sips of his coffee and chowing down the lasagna, and then took a call from the shop. When he stood up, he knocked the mug, the World's Greatest Dad mug I had bought for him one Christmas when I was little, onto the floor. "Shit, hold on a second Tommy. Dev," Dad said, covering the phone, "clean that up, will you please?"

Something that would have before made me cry—that ceramic mug smashing into huge chunks on the floor and Dad not making a big deal of it—now made me want to laugh. The World's Greatest Dad mug, *as if,* was destroyed.

Crouching down and picking up the thick pieces of ceramic, I realized then that no, my dad didn't know about the journal. Avo didn't tell him about what she did. Maybe, though, he also didn't want to know. True to form, doing anything to avoid talking to me about myself, my life, topics that didn't involve him.

Sitting back down at the table, I twirled my fork to break the connection of the pasta with the rest of the dish. This consistent avoidance made me feel more connected to my mother. I almost wanted to laugh a second time, as Dad continued checking his phone after he hung up with the shop, thinking how Avo said Dad would be home for supper, that we needed to spend time together. The only conversation we had, other than him telling me to pick up his mess, was when he told me to pass the salt.

I helped myself to seconds, continued staying quiet, waiting for the right time, while the birds chirped outside as they wound down for the night, all the while wanting to smash my dinner plate down on the ground. I trusted a cardinal would chirp at the feeder, my sign to tell me when to talk, when the right time came to share the information I now had at my fingertips. But none arrived.

After about ten minutes of playing this quiet game—this all-too-familiar game the Alante side of family played day after day, year after year, of knowing things between themselves, knowing lots of things, like information other people might want or need to know, information kept so close to the chest it was a wonder they could still breathe after this many years of not saying a word, never talking about a damn thing, at least not to my seventeen-year-old knowledge. With no cardinal showing up at the feeder, I decided on my next move. I would follow the Alante way, since that was half my blood, and keep the information from my mother's journals—how my father cheated, how my father physically treated my mother, and how she felt about it—to myself. For now.

CHAPTER SEVENTEEN

Hours later, after Dad showered and left to stay at Tina's, I sat back on my bed and read my mother's journal a second time. Then I flipped to a blank page in my own journal.

Mom. I stopped and held my pen mid-air, not entirely sure how to proceed, wondering if my thoughts, my ideas, my questions, were right and okay to ask, and what the consequences might be if they weren't.

Mom. It's me. Thanks for saying you loved me to pieces. That made me feel really nice.

Tears filled my eyes. I wiped them away, knowing I needed to stay focused in my request.

I'd like to ask you for a favor, I guess. If I'm right, and you sent me that dream about Dad—and I'm sorry if you wanted me to say something to him at supper, I will say something to him, I just don't know when, or how. I haven't figured that out yet, but it's going to be big and huge and a really important moment in my life, for obvious reasons. You know how he is more than I do, I suppose, so it has to be the right time. Even though I wanted to do it tonight, to yell at him for everything, everything I know about so far, I can't yet. Maybe that's why a sign never showed. I feel like I have something else I need to take care of first. And I'd like to ask for your help. It's about Gwen, my best friend, well, my former best friend it feels like, who you don't know, but maybe you do know her, if my feelings are right. She's with, well, I think you already know she's with someone who isn't good for her. So if you know that, and I suspect you do, because if she's my friend, you'd want to help her too, right? If that's true, would you send me another dream? One so I might help her?

I don't know how it works on the other side and I hope you don't feel like that's too much, my asking this, but if you're able to, would you tell me specifically, in a dream, what to do? I would really appreciate the help cause I honestly don't know what else to do at this point. It's kind of more than that, though. I mean, I want to be a good best friend and everything, but if I'm being honest and that's what journals are for (remember how you wrote that?) then the truth is that I have this thing called intuition and I think I'm pretty good at it, so good that I want to do it for a job someday. I think you can understand after what you wrote, and how you dream too—even though I don't know if they're the same kind of dreams as I have—that I want to do something other than work for Dad, or even go to college. I hope that's okay with you. I just don't think college is for me. I hope that doesn't let you down. I'm just not that kind of student, but I'm pretty good in these classes I'm taking at the police station. The thing is, I think I could be better. I know I could—if I didn't have these thoughts about Gwen and Andrew that keep coming into my head, distracting me. I feel like I have to take care of this first, then I can go and prove myself to the detectives at the station. That I can do this work. Even on a part-time basis, to actually do work I'm REALLY interested in would be awesome. There's really nothing else that I like or care about. The workshop instructor said I have to leave my stuff at the door, but I'm not able to do that right now, for whatever reason. I just can't let the Gwen thing go. But I want to. I need to. Cause I need to have a future using my intuition—it's the only thing I've ever really wanted— other than having you, my mother, here with me.

I dropped my pen down and cried, recalling the dream I had last year, right before Dad took me to the hospital to get Ativan. The dream that showed my mother standing shadow-like inside some Victorian, gothic-style home, mouthing the words, "I'm sorry."

My cries turned into sobbing, a sobbing so deep it stunned me I had so many tears to cry. I understood now. With my journal atop my shins, I cried until I couldn't cry anymore, my tears turning into a yawn. I looked at my clock, under the light of my lamp: 2:22 on Saturday morning—the sequence of numbers Gram used to always point out, beyond just the regular 11:11 time when everyone knew to make a wish.

Staring off in the dimly lit space of my bedroom, I closed my eyes and made my wish, right before falling into the deepest sleep I could ever remember.

CHAPTER EIGHTEEN

The moment I opened my eyes later that Saturday morning, adrenaline rushed through my body. Thoughts, memories, pictures, and images bombarded my brain like fireworks on the fourth of July. Slapping my hand around on the top of my comforter, I searched for my journal with my eyes still half closed, trying to retain every piece of information that had come to me during my dream state.

My pulse fast, excited, I scribbled down every detail I could remember. Then my phone buzzed, Frankie's name running across the screen.

Ideas and possibilities instantly flooded my brain.

"Good morning," I said, taking Frankie's call.

"S'up,—hold on a sec. Did you just say *good morning?*"

"I did," I said, continuing to write down what I could recall before the sound of Frankie's voice caused the dream remnants to fade.

I wasn't worried, though. I set down my pen and took a deep breath, pride bursting inside my chest, the way I always imagined other kids felt when they scored some kind of athletic or academic victory.

"Ah, would you care to expound?" Frankie said.

"Not at the moment," I answered, closing my journal. I picked up my mother's journal that had slept beside mine and squeezed it tight before stuffing both books under my mattress. "But I will ask you this, since you're the new party guy in town—anything fun happening tonight?"

"Now that just might be the weirdest question you've ever asked me in the history of our friendship," Frankie said as he flushed the toilet. "As a matter of fact, yes. Why?"

I pushed back the covers and got dressed. "Would the destination happen to be at Standish Park?" I asked.

"Well someone's been creeping on Instagram, even though they said they never would. As a matter of fact, Standish is a yes, since the donut superheroes have been all over the beach at night and we can't go there."

"Oh, no creeping here," I said, heading to the kitchen to make myself breakfast. "And since I want to work with those donut superheroes someday, are you going to call *me* that when I do? Anyway, what time are you picking me up?"

Frankie yelled something to his mom while I popped a slice of bread in the toaster. "Listen dude," he said, "if this is about Gwen, that ship has sailed. Why would you want to subject yourself to yet another episode of 'How stupid is Gwen'? You know what, why don't you and I both go somewhere else and have fun? It's a tri-town party anyway at Standish, which means Marshton hardos will be there, which means so will those two lovesick fools, even though I heard they were fighting again. I think we both could use a pick-me-up, seeing as Spanish class is not going so well for me at the moment, which means waaaay more than it should being that it's junior year. Why don't you just come over here and we'll watch some movies?"

I spread a thick layer of butter across the top of the light-brown toast. "Nope, tonight feels like the perfect party night to me. So, like I asked you before, what time are you picking me up?"

Frankie sighed. "Damn, girl. Sometimes I think you're a masochist, minus the sex part, or is that a sadist?"

"I'm neither. I just like to be right. And tonight, my friend, I'm going to prove I am."

CHAPTER NINETEEN

The night sky faded from a purple bruise hue to ink-like darkness as Frankie and I drove the two miles to Standish State Park. Everything felt dark to me as we took the side entrance into the forest, the one used for drug deals, for advanced hikers who knew what they were doing, and for partying teenagers who needed someplace to go.

Frankie's tires rolled over the dirt path and down the isolated road toward the old campground area. Only the stars offered a glimpse of light behind the thick evergreens lining the single-lane road. This part of the park apparently also represented the place where lovers cheated, according to the dream I had last night—the dream sent to me, from my mother, after I asked.

Apparently, the park was the very place my dad cheated on her, with that woman in the car.

The radio crackled, competing with static. My mother spared me the details in the dream, which I appreciated, but she showed me enough to confirm the first dream I had involving my two-timing father. More importantly, though, Mom had given me information about the future.

The scent of pine wafted in through both of the opened windows, smelling like Christmas. The dream actually felt like a Christmas gift. Cause if my hunches were right, the area was the approximate location where Andrew would cheat on Gwen. The dream also made logical sense too, with regard to the timing, since Frankie told me the two of them were fighting.

This time, though, I was going to catch him in the act.

No. *Gwen* would.

I sat in silence beside Frankie as we bumped and rolled over stones in the dirt. He lowered the volume of the radio after I shared with him about finding my mom's journal, the dream I had and, as a result, my plans tonight.

"I think this might be the first time I've been at a loss for words, my friend," Frankie said, both hands on the wheel as we continued down the winding road. "It's like your mother is communicating with you from heaven or something. I can't believe I just said that out loud."

I kept my eyes on the road. "Not *like*, I believe she is."

Frankie looked over at me, our faces mere shadows in the front seat. "You really think your mother answered you in your dream last night? Like actually heard your question and answered you?"

I raised one eyebrow while I pulled up Bobby Dempsey's number on my phone so I'd have it ready. "I know she did."

Frankie shook his head. "Crazy thing is—well, if we can add another crazy thing to the conversation, is that I believe you. Dude, if this night does go down the way you said it would, I'm going to start calling you boss lady."

I stared through the front windshield, attempting to catch sight of the crescent moon. "I'll take just being right and getting this whole night over with."

Headlights shone horizontally across the road several yards ahead of Frankie's Jetta. Cars eventually revealed themselves in dark shapes and sizes set back from the access road.

My legs started to shake.

I kept my hand on my phone, ready, whenever that might be, to contact Bobby—who, along with Len, had given me his contact information back when I worked on the Denise Franklin case, in the event that any other specific dream information came to me.

The Jetta bounced along the now rock-laden path, shocking the underside of the car. I felt a strange sensation in my chest. It was as if my chest expanded, an actual energy expanding past the parameters of my physical body. I felt the thrill of putting full faith in my mother—my mother who had passed away, who now resided on the other side.

The color black filled my mental screen as Frankie pulled beside the other twenty or so cars in the old campground lot. The pure darkness, a total void, allying with the shaking feeling in my legs—a feeling of when you don't know your next move, or how to navigate, almost frozen. For a second, doubt crept in. *Is this really going to happen and should I even be here?*

I gripped the door handle for a moment and got out of the car. Noticing some of his friends, Frankie immediately started goofing around. I felt relieved in his distraction. I needed to focus and tune in to figuring out the steps to take.

Trust. The word had come to me when I awoke after dreaming. *Trust your senses.*

This spoke to me now.

I closed my eyes, hearing the banter of teenagers around me, feeling my heart rev up inside my chest. I hoped I'd be able to trust myself, my gut, my clairvoyant or clairsentient or clairaudient mind, whichever method was going to show up to guide me on what to do. The only thing I knew right at that moment was this: That Andrew would be with that blond girl with the belly ring, they would be in the car I saw in my dream, and he was very definitely going to betray Gwen.

Standing beside Frankie at the trunk of some kid's car, I assessed the scene as best I could in the dark, the headlights of a few vehicles the only light with which to see. Groups of kids gathered beside, between, and around the back of three rows of cars and pick-up trucks I didn't recognize.

I scratched at my leg, doubt seeping into my brain a second time. What if I got the night wrong? What if Andrew wasn't here?

My eyes darted back and forth. What if Gwen wasn't even here, and if Andrew did end up doing something wrong, she wouldn't be able to witness it, and we'd be back to square one? What if this was some wild goose chase and I wound up with nothing, driving home with Frankie after my failed strategy, ending up as some kind of masochist after all?

I squeezed my fists and inhaled, remembering the part of the dream where Gwen saw it, all right . . . she *really saw.* It was the moment she would come to realize her relationship with Andrew had been a disaster of a mistake.

Right. I had to remember that. I saw Gwen vividly in the dream.

I know she's here, I thought to myself, *and if she isn't yet, she will be.*

I bit down on my lip. If I couldn't trust my mother's information, then truly, I had nothing.

I glanced down at my phone. Bobby's contact information stared back at me. My pulse raced and I tucked the phone in the back pocket of my shorts.

"Hey, guys," Gwen said, somewhat cheerily, coming over to Frankie and me, as if we all hadn't just gone a week without speaking.

"Give me one of those," I whispered to Frankie. He handed me a beer from the back of his friend's trunk with a confused look on his face. Then he grabbed a bottle of water from a separate small cooler, knowing I would have killed him if he drank and drove.

"Hey," I said. I half-waved, following her lead and acting like nothing had happened to our friendship.

"Hey, G," Frankie said, giving her a half-hearted hug. He looked at me guiltily, making me feel both awful and good at the same time. Awful because part of me still didn't want to hurt Gwen, or see her get hurt, and good because I could tell Frankie believed everything was going to go down exactly, or at least close to, the way I said it would. That gave me more confidence.

"You're drinking?" Gwen asked me, her nose wrinkled. She swayed a bit, and I knew she was buzzed.

I brought the full bottle to my lips, trying not to wince at the nasty taste. "Oh, you know, just one," I said, taking the tiniest of sips. "Frankie's rubbing off on me."

Frankie chuckled and continued talking to his friend, avoiding the fake conversation Gwen and I were about to have.

"Are you still mad at me?" Gwen said with her eyes at half-mast.

"You gotta do you, Gwen," I said. I spilled half my beer into the matted-down grass, knowing she wouldn't notice. "It's all good."

She glanced back at the tennis girls she had driven here with and then said to me, "Let's just agree to disagree about the Andrew thing. I'm sure this doesn't surprise you or anything, but I'm mad at him again. I hope he shows up, though. I didn't tell him I'd be here." She turned away again, looking for any sign of Andrew. She spotted his crew hanging out behind someone's car a row over. Andrew, though, appeared nowhere in sight.

Chills ran down my spine and I pulled my hands inside the sleeves of my sweatshirt.

Gwen weaved through the crowd with purpose. "Hey," she said to one of the kids with his hat turned backward. "Is Andrew with you?"

I watched the group of six guys look at one another for direction, which I didn't know if Gwen caught, due to the state she was in. "Oh, I think he had to go to the bathroom or something. Is that where he is, guys?" one of them asked the others.

Jared stepped back from the circle and snickered, "Yeah, that's it. That's where he is."

Gwen pulled her arms in tighter to her chest. "Okay, well, if you see him . . . I know you probably already know we aren't talking and everything, but if you see him, tell him I'm here, okay?"

One of the guys looked Gwen up and down in both a nod to her beauty but also, I sensed, how pathetic and dumb girls can be. "Okay, we will," he said, which seemed to satisfy Gwen, for she turned on her heels and made her way back over to me.

My throat tightened, thinking about how Dad must have behaved with his friends back in the day.

"I have to pee, will you go with me?" Gwen asked, leaning in close. "I need to find somewhere private so someone doesn't post it. It's so embarrassing when they do that." I could smell the alcohol on her breath and knew that maybe she truly did have to go to the bathroom, but that she also probably wanted to find Andrew.

Showtime.

Tempted to dial Bobby's number right then, so everything would fall into place, I took my phone back out of my pocket, the adrenalin rush back, pulsing in my veins. Then I paused. I was about to rescue Gwen from a relationship she might have stayed in for the rest of her life—and she had no clue.

"Sure, I have to go too," I lied. My stomach felt queasy. I needed to lead Gwen to the area where my dreams revealed I needed to be. But where was that, exactly?

I stood in the lot and closed my eyes to feel a sense of direction. I tried to quiet my mind over Luke Combs playing from someone's car radio. A tug on my left side pulled me toward the deeper forest.

"Here we go," I whispered to Frankie, out of Gwen's earshot.

"Do you want me to come with you?" he whispered back, clutching my arm, while Gwen continued to glance around, desperately searching for Andrew.

"Stay here," I said, right before saying a quick prayer to be able to follow the details of the aerial view I was shown in my dream, the one where Frankie hung back near his car while Gwen and I went into the woods—somewhere deep, yet not that deep. Somewhere I wasn't privy to yet.

I pretended I was buzzed. Which felt pretty easy to do, laughing and tripping once in awhile over roots in the ground at the same time spilling out my beer until there was barely any left, as I led Gwen into the dense area of trees. Acting drunk felt like the best thing to do since I could just blame it on the alcohol when we "accidentally" found Andrew. That is, if I didn't feel brave enough to announce at the top of my lungs once we busted him, "See what I've been saying? Finally! You get it now!"

One small path led to another, and we ended up in front of a small stream.

Nerves shot through me. I didn't recall any type of stream, or body of water of any kind, in my dream. We weren't in the right place. I just didn't know where to go from there.

I took a deep breath and turned left, cutting through dense brush, while sticks and branches scratched against my ankles.

"Oh my God, where are we?" Gwen laughed, the alcohol clearly in full effect. She waved the flashlight of her phone zig-zaggedly across the green ground cover as we moved farther into the woods, farther away from the party. The music now faded from earshot. "I hope we find our way back. I also hope I don't get poison ivy. You'll have to shine the light on the ground when I go."

I glanced back, no longer able to see Frankie's car. My hands shook. I wasn't sure we'd find our way back, either, which, at that point, was the lesser of two evils. If we took too long to find what my dream wanted me to, I'd miss the opportunity altogether, and maybe even get poison ivy on top of the fail.

"Sure, I'll shine the light for you," I said, telling Gwen whatever she wanted to hear. I held the now-empty bottle of beer in my hand and tried to control my breathing and focus my mind, asking for a sign as to the right way to go next as we crept deeper into the forest. I needed some area, some landmark that looked slightly familiar from the dream.

We passed large tree after large tree, making me feel like Hansel and Gretel, a story that had always freaked me out and made me feel sad when the kids felt far from their mother, far from home. My throat felt dry. I asked not to lose the opportunity of the moment, to not waste more time as no sign from my dream emerged. I almost felt as if I might faint. I prayed, one last time—as Gwen sang some song behind me and took selfies on her phone—that I'd control my sudden panic and find what my dreams said I would by coming to this party tonight.

A few more minutes of traipsing through ground cover went by. Then, like someone physically placed their hands on the back of my neck, my head turned left, without any reasoning on my part.

I squinted, seeing only darkness.

Go forward. There.

I heard this in my mind, but it was as if someone stood right next to me and spoke the words. Goosebumps covered my body.

Maybe I just imagined it. Or maybe I heard and felt it.

I froze, trying to figure out what was real or what I might have imagined, while also trying not to waste another second as Gwen kept asking me why we were going farther, telling me, exasperatingly now, that she could just go to the bathroom right where we were and that she was done walking to find a good spot already.

Fear rose inside me like a thermometer. Though I knew it was too late to turn back now.

Keep going.

I steadied myself as I let the words from that other place sink in.

Mom? Is that you talking to me or is it my own mind, my own thoughts?

I wanted to hear the words again, to see if they sounded female, but there was no time for that.

"Dev, we're in way too deep," Gwen said. "I'm just going to go right here."

That's when, a few feet ahead, I saw a barely visible footpath.

Energy gathered in my throat—a swirl like that exact weather pattern that needs to happen in order to create the perfect storm.

The footpath appeared eerily similar to the one I saw in my dream, with the green ground cover lining its winding curves. It was incredible to me that I could see something in real time that I had previously seen in my bedroom, while I was sleeping.

I hit the flashlight app on my phone and shined it several feet in front of me.

"Hold on, there's a clearing up ahead, let's go there so you won't get poison ivy," I said, half-lying about my intentions.

"At this point, I don't care. You're freaking me out with how far we're going into the woods. I'm going here," Gwen said. She squatted down behind me in an area of thick brush.

Breathe.

I continued walking, in an almost obsession-like state, toward the dream clearing I had been shown but couldn't yet see, and toward the pine trees in my dream that towered around that clearing, and the signpost that stuck out of the grass indicating some landmark in the woods discovered by some boy scout troops or hikers on their way to some milestone, and toward the gray car that my dream showed me parked in the clearing, eventually revealing the reason for my mission tonight. All in some place I had never been, never seen in real-life, but saw so vividly in the dream, that it was almost like I had already been here.

And that's when I saw the scene for real.

Saw it with my own two eyes, while Gwen stood up from the brush and re-buttoned her shorts in relief.

Except, instead of a gray car sitting in the small clearing fifty feet away, like the car my dreams had showed me, there was a gray-shingled, dilapidated little wooden shed. A shed highlighted by the slight contrast of a 4 x 4 foot, fogged-up window.

I stepped closer, some instinctive, magnetic pull leading me toward my dream manifestation. When I got within five feet of the foggy window, dimly light inside from someone's phone, Gwen trailing behind me continuing to ask where the hell we were going and what was wrong with me, I saw moving shadows. Two moving shadows that made grunting sounds.

"Oh my God, of all places," Gwen said, with her nose curled. "That's so gross!"

Like a robot, I raised my phone and shone the flashlight directly inside the shed.

That's when I heard a gasp in Gwen's throat, a strained gurgle sound like when someone is in pain.

Unable to speak, I stood staring through the glass at the chubby, blond girl with the messy bun spilling all over her head and the stiffening posture of a sweaty, bare-chested, entirely stunned Andrew.

CHAPTER TWENTY

"I hate you! I hate you!" Gwen screamed, so loud I thought she'd lose her voice.

The door burst open and slammed the outside of the shed. "It's not what you think!" Andrew said. He fidgeted with the button on his jeans, T-shirt haphazardly slung over his bare shoulder, yelling, "I'm drunk, I didn't know what I was doing!"

I observed Andrew's last-ditch attempt to manipulate Gwen into thinking he was one of the good guys and then texted Bobby in somewhat of a trance. Feeling guided by a force that seemed to be reminding me of what I now needed to do in that moment—letting him know that it was me, Devon, that I needed his help right now, some out-of-control party at Standish Park that required the police.

Even in the trance I knew I risked looking like a fool. If it all didn't play out the way I saw things happen in my dream, I gambled with Bobby getting into trouble too, taking him away from where he was supposed to be during his regular shift. I did it anyway. I had to. Every piece of me, the strong pieces, the dazed pieces, the hoping and praying pieces, needed to trust the dream guidance I received.

I blinked in the darkness. Andrew tried to grab Gwen's shoulders, to get her to listen, to reason with him and why he might be in a shed in the woods with some girl that wasn't his girlfriend. But Gwen didn't stand still, didn't allow him the time to speak.

Instead, she ran.

She ran back toward the party, tripping over thick forestation and dead branches, all the while Andrew calling behind her, "Wait, will you? I love you! You know I love you. She didn't mean anything to me! She's the town whore—everyone knows it!"

"I hope you get in a car accident and die, you scumbag motherfucker!" Gwen yelled as she ran, at the same time crying like I had never seen her cry in all the years I'd known her.

I texted Frankie, telling him to watch for Gwen, that *it* happened, and he needed to be there. I stayed put in the clearing for another minute, ignoring the blond "town whore" in her too-small shorts and white-knit half-sweater, revealing the silver-hoop belly ring I didn't need any more as evidence as she cowered past me, using her flashlight to find her way back to her friends.

The haze that had been around me began to melt. It had been five minutes with no reply from Bobby. Maybe he wasn't working. I heard an owl hoot in the distance. If that were the case, I wouldn't have the help I thought I'd have, from the police, and the night still wasn't over yet. I needed to get back to Gwen.

I picked up my pace, hurrying back to the party as the noise of the crowd, including shouting between Gwen and Andrew, grew louder. Minutes later, before I even reached the entrance to the path, I saw the crowd had gathered in a jagged circle.

I made my way around the unevenly parked cars to where Gwen and Andrew stood in the middle of the circle, screaming at each other. He had his hand gripped around her arm, telling everyone who stood there watching to "get the fuck away from them and let him talk to his girlfriend in private." Gwen held her face in her hands and cried.

Meanwhile, my body grew cold. I watched as Andrew's eyes narrowed—even smaller than his usual creepy stare—his body moving quickly, desperately, like a fox caught in a trap. Even Jared, standing back with the Marshton crew on the other side of the circle, watched with baited breath to see how far Gwen would go, and whether she'd fall prey again to Andrew's lies, as the two of them continued to argue in the middle of the circle.

A moment later, with her puffy eyes and tear-stained face, Gwen leaned in close to Andrew's face, yet spoke loudly enough for everyone to hear. "I can't wait until I'm with someone else—maybe even one of your good-looking friends. Thanks for teaching me everything I need to know."

Wild-eyed, Andrew grabbed her face, hard, like crinkling a paper bag, and shoved Gwen to the ground. "You're just like every other girl I know," he spat, his face venomous and dark.

Silent, everyone stood still, as if unable to move, until one of Andrew's friends stepped forward. "Dude," the kid started to say.

Then, out of nowhere, Andrew hauled off and kicked Gwen in her side. There was a sudden gasp, a sharp inhale, the crowd in almost disbelief as the true character of Andrew—not just a cheater, but a violent cheater—was revealed.

That's when I lost it.

I pounced on Andrew, whaling the back of him with my fists, Andrew suddenly morphing into, becoming, my father.

I said things under my breath I don't remember saying, feeling things I didn't remember feeling until Frankie, and other guys from both Hanley and Marshton, peeled me off Andrew, and then worked to peel Andrew off Gwen.

At some point, in the mix of all this, the cops arrived. Dusty and sweaty, I suddenly found myself watching a Hanley police officer holding Frankie back from Andrew, and another officer handcuffing Andrew's wrists.

Beside the police cruiser, Gwen's tennis friends wrapped a blanket around her, while every other Hanley teenager pointed to Andrew, identifying him as the one who started the whole thing and that, "Obviously, he had serious anger management issues."

After the situation got under control, Bobby came over and took my face in his hands, like he was conducting an evaluation for a concussion. "Are you all right?"

I stared back into his gentle, yet concerned eyes, my body shaking with everything that just happened. To Gwen, but also everything that had happened before—to my mother. In another place and time, I might have liked Bobby's hands caressing the bottom half of my face. In that moment, though, I simply appreciated his trying to get me to focus on my feet, and where I was standing.

"I'm okay," I said in a quiet voice, not sure if I was or I wasn't.

The blue lights swirled intensely above the cruiser. When he seemed satisfied with my answer, Bobby patted me on the shoulder and then checked on Gwen. After Bobby took down his report, I heard him encourage Gwen to talk to her parents and that the police would likely be in touch with them too, because she was under eighteen.

Andrew pleaded with the officer who opened the back door of the cruiser. "Ask my friends!" Andrew countered, his voice choked with emotion. "I got jumped from two Hanley guys, go ask them!"

"Shut up, you moron," Frankie called over his shoulder on his way to stand next to me. "Game over."

The other, balding officer turned to Jared and company standing beside the cop car. "You want to say something to help your friend? Did he really get jumped?"

Andrew directed a pained stare at his friends. "Go ahead, tell them how those guys jumped me for no reason."

One of the kids stretched his chin toward the sky in a slight nervous twitch, considering for a second that he might catch crap for it later. He shook his head, "C'mon man, you hit your girlfriend."

Andrew laughed out loud, a condescending laugh, his eyes darting back and forth between his friends. "What are you talking about? You saw those guys!"

Jared scuffed at the ground. "You kicked her, kid, just shut up already."

Even though dating definitely wasn't in our future, I made a mental note to say hi to Jared the next time I saw him around, that is, if I ever decided to go to another party.

"Let's go, my friend," the officer said. He stuffed Andrew's stocky frame into the back seat.

"You sure you're good?" Bobby asked me again, after Frankie confirmed that yes, Andrew was the one who hit Paul Callahan down at the beach that night and that he'd take me home, making sure I was okay.

I nodded, thanked him for responding to my text that I never even saw until after it was all over. I told him I'd see him Thursday night in the final class and that really, everything was fine.

A few minutes later, after most of the cars had gone and the alcohol was dumped, Bobby drove away, watching me for a moment out of the passenger-side window before he turned to talk to his partner.

I followed the taillights as Frankie and I stepped across the flattened down, grassy lot toward Gwen.

"Don't say anything," she said. She avoided looking at Frankie and me as the tennis girls got in a Toyota Highlander.

"Are you okay?" I asked. I tasted a smudge of dirt on my lip and wiped it away with my sleeve.

Gwen bowed her head. "I'm so stupid," she said, her hands clutching at her stomach.

Frankie crouched down to look at her face. "Who cares? The kid's a douche. It's over."

"You're not stupid," I said. "You're the least stupid person I know."

"No, you can say it. I am stupid," Gwen said, her voice quivering. "I just want to be left alone."

"Gwen," I said, wanting desperately for her to know that my mother was watching out for her as much as I was. "Listen. I had another vision and it showed me the party and . . . "

"I said don't talk to me," she said, her body trembling visibly in the red taillights of her friend's car. "Wait, you knew and went with me in the woods anyway, knowing what we'd find?"

I furrowed my brow. "You're mad at *me?*"

Gwen gripped her elbows, as if she was trying to cover her body from being exposed. "Is that why you're here? Oh my God, I really am stupid. You hate parties. You hate people in general, you don't even like waiting on customers at Holly's."

Frankie lowered his voice so as not to cause Gwen further embarrassment in front of her other friends who called out the back window, asking if she was ready to leave. "Dude, are you seriously mad at Dev?"

"You put your visions over our friendship?" Gwen asked. She looked at me, tears streaming down her face. "I just got humiliated in front of kids from two schools. I can't wait to see all the social media blowing up in my face. And now you too?"

"I didn't want you to be humiliated, and I didn't put my visions over our friendship. I'm here *because of our friendship.*"

Gwen scoffed and opened the back door of the car. "Just leave me alone."

"She'll come around. Give her time," Frankie said as we drove down the bumpy, isolated road toward home. "As a complete aside, I never saw you get so mad before, girl—the way you jumped on Andrew's back like that, all one hundred seventeen pounds of you. That must have been how your dad got in fights back in the day." He gently pushed my shoulder. "It's good you got your anger out on the right person. Cause I wouldn't want it to be me."

I chuckled at Frankie's attempt to brighten my mood, staring out the front windshield at the vast, dark void. For a second, I almost felt sorry for Andrew in a way that took me by surprise, since I was his biggest hater. I realized it was similar to how I felt kind of sorry for my father, after I read my mom's journals, knowing my dad wasn't all bad—he could be a good person, too, since he had raised me basically on his own and I turned out okay. And he had to have loved my mother, I thought, even when he cheated, like maybe he was just young and dumb or couldn't help himself, the way kids my age drink and vape cause they don't think about getting cancer or liver disease later.

"Talk about getting things right in your dream," Frankie said. He shook his head as he turned on his high beams. "That is some epic shit."

I searched for the Big Dipper in the sky, wondering if Gwen would ever forgive me, if she'd ever understand why I did what I did. "Do you think I did the right thing?" I asked Frankie. "I needed to show her what he's all about, right, to protect her from getting hurt in the future and everything? Also, I didn't get the car part right. I saw a gray car in my dream. There wasn't a car in the clearing, only a gray shed."

Frankie looked over at me like I had three heads as the car rolled over a bump. "Are you serious? First of all, yes, you did the right thing. Helllloooo. You're a good friend, D. And gray car, gray shed, who the eff cares! You nailed it! From the blond girl to the night and place it happened. I think the donut superheroes, sorry, the cops, would be impressed. You'll be working for them in no time, Ms. Alante."

CHAPTER TWENTY-ONE

Thursday night at the station, on the final night of the remote viewing class, I answered Gloria that yes, I had been sleeping better, and then settled in the cold, hard, yet perfectly comfortable plastic seat, my shoulders back, posture straight. Though I felt pressured to prove to Allison that I could make it in the advanced class, I felt a lot more confident after my dream, and what had gone down last weekend. I also felt better—even after not hearing from Gwen all week or seeing any social media posts that might reveal she was okay and that we were, in fact, still friends—since I dropped off a letter to her right before I biked, on time, to class.

In the three-page letter, I told Gwen how I found my mother's journals. I shared the similarities I felt between Andrew and my father in ways that freaked me out and how I asked my mom for help about Gwen's situation. I was only trying to protect her, I explained in my neatest penmanship, and that I hoped we could still be the best of friends.

Allison, called out of the room for a moment, instructed Lisa to pass out pencils and paper to those already seated, in preparation for the final class exercise. I listened to the hum of the air conditioning unit in the back of the room, knowing I had done what I could. Gwen would read the letter on her own time and decide whether or not to understand where I was coming from. That part was up to her. I had to let it go.

I tucked my phone under my seat, ready to focus, now that I could. Tonight's class exercise was my last shot to have some kind of success so that Allison or Len, or whoever decided my fate after the workshop ended, would know for certain that this work was something I definitely wanted, and planned, to continue. I didn't plan to scoop ice cream, or work for my father, the rest of my life.

"Hey," Bobby said. He nimbly slid between Ben's chair and my own before he sat down beside me in his usual seat closest to the wall. He ignored Walter's sarcastic comment about straggling in close to start time and pulled his seat closer to the table, his sneaker brushing against my foot. "Everything good with your friend? And with you?"

"Thanks to you guys," I said. The students chatted amongst themselves while we waited for Allison. "I haven't talked to Gwen in almost a week, but it'll be okay."

Bobby leaned over his clasped hands, that all-business yet cool and warm way he had that I liked. "Just curious, did you know before it happened?"

We briefly locked eyes. "Something like that," I said. Why bother trying to make up something else to say? I needed all my energy tonight for whatever practice exercise we were given.

Bobby looked at me again, searching for something, like he had when I talked to him that night at the beach. "Nice. You'll have to tell me more about that sometime. Like I said, I'm interested."

Warmth spread through my body. "Cool. Maybe I will." Since we had time and I wanted to keep the conversation going, I added, "What's not so cool is that I feel like Gwen didn't think I was being a good friend, even though I was being a good friend, from my perspective. Do you know what I mean?" I heard myself talking to Bobby more like a friend than a colleague. I wondered if that was okay, if I had crossed a line. I wondered if maybe I was looking for someone else, too, other than Frankie, to tell me I had done the right thing.

Bobby nodded, like he understood. "She got her heart broken, even if it was from a loser. She'll thank you later. I'm just glad you're okay. We need you to flex your skills tonight, show these old guys up."

I was still smiling even after Bobby sat back in his chair once Allison returned, thanking us for our patience. I never had someone, especially a guy somewhat close to my age, yet older too, talk to me like that—in a way that was, well, mature.

"Tonight," Allison said, adjusting the hem of her tailored blazer, "we have a real-life challenge we'll be needing your resources on. An actual case has just come into the department."

My heart skipped a beat. Excitement burst inside me, exploding with the message that if I did well, on whatever type of problem they were asking us to solve, it would probably carry more weight, since it mattered in real life, not some previously solved case tucked away in some folder. A pain seared in my side. What if I didn't do well? That would make it worse, if I proved I couldn't work under pressure.

Allison cleared her throat. "The situation involves a seventeen-year-old female possible runaway. We'll call her 'S.' And that's all you get. I'm not going to give you any more of the department details because there are officers currently working on the case in a regular procedural sense. And that's all you get because the less a remote viewer is given ahead of time, the better. Your job is to use the skills you've learned here over the past three weeks to see what's revealed *to you* in that multisensory way."

"Can you tell us if there's possible drug use or the child's social media habits?" George asked, pushing his glasses up on his face. I pushed aside the "child" reference even though the girl was seventeen, like me, out of my mind to stay focused on the task at hand.

"Or at least more about the type of kid she is and who she hangs out with," Walter said, sitting with his arms crossed.

"Sorry," Allison said. "I've given you all you need. Your job is to *inform me,* after we take a few minutes to quiet our minds, whatever details *come to you,* whatever else the department might need to know, from a different perspective, in order to solve the case."

Bobby's slightly tanned forehead wrinkled in thought. I closed my eyes, wanting to get quiet even before Allison started the meditation, to make the most use of my time.

Taking in a big, deep breath, I asked Mom to guide me. Now that I didn't have to think about Gwen and Andrew anymore—well, maybe stewing a little bit on how Gwen wasn't talking to me, but not in the way it had been before—there was lightness surrounding me this time around. I felt ease in beginning the exercise. Clairvoyantly, I felt a gentle wind move through me, whispering a message of how I wasn't clogged up, filled with preoccupied thoughts anymore, and that maybe things might come to me easier now because of that freedom of mind.

Exhaling, I waited. My mental screen dark, a blank slate. I inhaled and exhaled two more times, to settle into the right position, the right chord, in order to receive the flow of information I needed. Information to help the department, yes, but as my heart rate sped up and colors began sparking in my mind in firework fashion, I realized, what I really felt compelled to do was *help the girl.*

My body felt on fire. No, it felt electric. It was as if as soon as I thought about the girl, and not about what the department needed me to do, or what I wanted to do for myself, in order to prove my worth and pull my weight, my body responded, connecting with the truth. No, my intuition responded. It came alive. Suddenly, colors, feelings, images, words—so many ways of receiving showed in my brain like one of those city grid maps, details being delivered to me all at once.

I remembered what Gloria said when we worked together in the last class, how to tell the information to slow down. *Help me remember it all, help me to make sense of everything you're showing me,* I whispered silently to my mind.

Like shifting into first gear, I instructed the thoughts, the rapid-fire data to slow down, to pause on a freeze frame, if that made sense. I trusted my intuition would understand what I was asking. I didn't want to miss a thing.

Without a partner, the information was a little harder to retain because I knew I still had to write stuff down when I was finished. A thought dropped down into my mind like an anchor— if I was ever asked, I would let someone know I preferred to work with a partner. That way *they* could record the session while I spoke. The steady stream of information that came to me could then fall into someone else's hands, so they, as the detective or whoever I was assigned to, could do something with it. I realized *my job, my strength, was simply to witness, to see.*

Fast thoughts soared across my brain. The partner had to be someone who wouldn't judge me, someone who would allow me to talk freely, trusting my responses and writing down the data the way it came to me as the remote viewer. This thought followed by yet another one . . . that someday I would love to work with Bobby in that way, if I ever got the opportunity.

"All right everyone," Allison said after time subsided. "Fifteen minutes are up. Write down what you received, as legibly as possible, please, since someone outside the class will be reviewing the data this evening."

I wrote neatly yet furiously as Allison turned on the lights, as if my life depended on it, in a way I never had on any test in high school. I never looked at Bobby to my right, or Ben to my left, or cared about Walter or Ed looking at me after they had written down a couple of things and then spent the rest of the time looking around the room, making a few hushed comments under their breath about how intense those of us who were still working appeared.

Allowing the remainder of those writing a few more minutes, Allison glanced at her watch. "Write your name at the top and forward your papers to the end of the row."

"Would you normally get more time to do something like this?" Pete asked, tucking his pencil in the pocket of his dress shirt.

"Yes," Allison answered. "Remote viewing sessions usually go for forty-five minutes to an hour. Most viewers I've worked with tend to go no more than ninety minutes of that intensely focused time. The purpose of the fifteen minutes was to fit in the rest of what we needed tonight—being the final class—while also being able to assemble data for the department in a timely fashion for a timely situation. I also wanted to show off my students' skills to gain support from the department for this work. In my opinion, after these few weeks, we have valuable resources here for assistance on future cases."

"I think I'll stick to the regular tactics as a good old-fashioned regular detective," Walter said. Then, glancing over his shoulder at me while I continued writing, he added, "I'll be interested to see if these young kids who've been writing like a fiend come up with anything that'll make a difference to a live case."

I lifted my chin, put down my pencil, and prayed that my filled page of phrases and little drawings explaining what I saw and felt and heard made sense to whoever viewed my data.

"How do they understand what we wrote if we didn't even understand it?" Lisa asked.

Allison appeared bemused. "Supervisors have been trained to view the collected data for patterns and themes. Remember, your job isn't to necessarily interpret or understand the information. Your job as an intuitive viewer is to open your mind in an entirely different, non-local conscious way so that you can receive content by other means—other means and perspectives that could be the key to solving a case."

Ed crossed his arms over his chest. "I'm with Walter. I don't know how this new-age tactic is going to change anything we've done as a department and done well, I might add, for the better."

Gloria laughed behind me and Allison gave her a knowing look, surprisingly displaying a bit of her personality beyond the professional demeanor she normally kept. Probably, I figured, because of it being the last class. She shrugged, "If I haven't convinced you guys by now, I'm not going to. We'll have to see if results from our group speak for themselves, if anything is revealed tonight. I told the supervisors on the case that if any data does prove relevant, it would be good feedback for us as a class. In the meantime, let's take a five-minute break before finishing up with the curriculum."

Bobby nudged my elbow while everyone else grabbed coffee and checked their phones. "Want to compare notes? Though I think you wrote a lot more down than I did."

"Sure," I said, thinking this would be a good distraction from my growing obsessive thought that we might not find out anything at all about the case, being the last class. I chewed on my lip. Is that how it worked—you just gave the police your data and might never find out how you did? How could you work like that, without any feedback like we got during the exercises?

"I'll go first," Bobby said, keeping his voice low. "I saw a first-floor window and then some woods. I saw a guy, but I don't know if that was her boyfriend, or some lunatic trying to lure her out the window after meeting her on social media or something. I don't know. I couldn't really get a good read on the guy—he seemed older to me than a boyfriend. I don't know if my thoughts just automatically went to the whole social-media-stalking thing, with all the workshops we've taken. Anyway, that's all I got. You get anything similar so I can feel hopeful over here?"

I had been listening intensely, staring at the floor. Finding I loved the process, the discussion, the comparing of notes—until my face blushed after what Bobby said. I looked up and smiled, even though I reasoned he was probably trying to make me feel better after my failed attempts at success—and that the success I did have wasn't simply a case of beginner's luck.

"I got woods too," Gloria said, interrupting our conversation.

"Yeah, but what woods?" Bobby asked, glancing back at Gloria and then back at me. "I didn't get any specific area, so not sure how you could go on that."

Gloria adjusted her reading glasses. "True. If a few of us got woods as a piece of information, though, it might present as a theme. They could perhaps search woods in the general vicinity."

"Unless she's already in an area far from home," Bobby said. He tapped the eraser of his pencil against the desk. "Did you get anything else, Gloria?" I liked how he thought enough to say her name. Respectful. Walter and Ed wouldn't have the courtesy to do that.

"Other than the girl's name being Siobhan or an Irish name like that, that's the only piece of information I received. My husband was up all night with the spring flu; I get a pass."

My pulse quickened. That girl must be so scared, if that was the situation—like she got abducted or something. I thought about what other thoughts might be racing through the girl's mind—what thoughts I'd have, if it was me. I rotated my ankle twice to bring myself back. That's when I noticed Bobby and Gloria's eyes on me, waiting for me to share what I received.

An excitement pulsed through my veins, mixed with a feeling of belonging. "I saw the woods too," I said. I paused, careful not to sound too excited. "I also got a few letters, G and R, but I don't know if they were related to the woods or the situation in general. I saw a house with two floors, grandparents watching TV in the lower level, then a car in the gravel driveway, a Pontiac Firebird, old car, driven by a guy, but unfortunately I never saw him—I'd give him the age thirty-two, though. Maybe the letter D for the name, but I don't know if that was connected to the woods part. He definitely didn't know her personally, meaning in her life at school or a family friend or anything, so I'd say the social media thing fits. I got the name Saoirse, so the Irish name thing hit for me too, Gloria. I also saw the girl's jeans, torn at the knee, not on purpose like a fashion style, more like ripped in an attempt to flee. Not a good situation, that's for sure. Anyway, that's it." I took what I hoped was a silent breath, to steady myself and not to come off like I had gotten more information that they did. Meanwhile, I had no idea if anything made sense at all, since it didn't make sense to me, which either meant it was really specifically right or really stupid and totally wrong.

"Well done," Gloria said, after a moment. "Now I really hope they have feedback for us before we end. Then we can see if we got some hits."

Bobby was silent, his eyes staring into mine. His stare went right through me, somewhere deeper than where I simply sat in my chair. Though I never felt like a boundary line more than friendship—or workship, I guess you'd call it—was crossed between us. It seemed to me to be more of a fascination he had with this whole remote viewing thing, for some reason I wasn't privy to.

"What?" I finally asked, my cheeks turning pink.

Bobby blinked and drew a little circle on the table with his eraser. "There's a park in the town over in Rockton, where I live, called the George Rayham Park, named after a veteran my family knew years ago. It's a small place, but everyone in town knows it."

"Really?" I asked. I touched my necklace.

He nodded, glancing briefly at the dragonfly around my neck and then returning his gaze to mine, as if doing an interrogation.

"Well, we don't even know if I'm right, you know, if the information is right," I said. I bounced my leg against the chair, silently praying inside my mind that it would be.

"I didn't say you were right," Bobby said, with a side smile. "But it'd be pretty cool if you were."

———

The rest of the two-hour class, though interesting in terms of summarizing the information we had learned over the past four weeks, didn't carry the same weight it had initially. This was likely due to the fact that I was crawling out of my skin with wanting to know what had happened to that girl—if my information was right, if S was okay. And where the information came from, anyway? Was it that same place that it always came from, or this time did it come from my mother?

A tingling occurred against my skin. Was it Mom every time? Or did she only send me the stuff on Gwen because she wanted Gwen to get away from Andrew, because something bad might happen, because she understood and didn't want Gwen to live her life with a cheater?

I closed my eyes and took a few deep breaths, trying to control all the overwhelming feelings building inside my chest. In the midst of my thoughts, I touched Bobby's ankle with my foot by accident. I drew my legs under my chair as close as I could to myself. I hoped to God he didn't think I did that on purpose.

Over the next ten minutes, only half of me heard Allison explain how she'd let everyone know by email within the next two weeks whether or not they were going to be taking the advanced class over the summer—and for those not interested, to let her know so a slot could open for someone else, since the department agreed to pay for only five participants. The other half of me prayed to Mom, Gram, and Archangel Michael that I would end up being right on the S case—an *actual* case—so they'd have no choice but to ask me back and help me develop my skills, unless, of course, due to my age, they automatically didn't plan on including me.

I bit my thumbnail. In the midst of my thoughts, someone knocked on the door and asked Allison to step in the hall for a few minutes.

"Reckoning time," Walter called out once Allison left the room. "Time to see if the taxpayer's money for this class paid off."

I clasped my hands and pressed them hard against my mouth, trying to assess the shadowy movement through the rectangular frosted window in the conference room door. After a few minutes, Allison re-entered the room, checking her watch. "Well, as they say, you save the best for last." She suppressed a smile. "Let's end with some positives, shall we? First and foremost, the girl was found, safely, thank goodness, and primarily unharmed, though the situation could have been worse, as it involved a predatory social media situation."

Bobby and I glanced at each other and then turned our attention back to the front of the room to hear Allison's full report.

"Though we can't give names of the parties involved, the girl was found in an area called the George Rayham Park, a few towns over from here, I believe. She tried to get away from the perpetrator at one point, ripping her jeans on a low barbed wire fence, when some hikers had shown up, thankfully. The man, who didn't know S other than chatting online, is currently in custody in the town of Abingdale. After the detectives finish the full report, S will be going home with her grandparents, who have full custody due to both her parents being out of the picture. Now, even though they apprehended the perpetrator and the victim without our data, they were very interested in several of the findings from our group. They were able to see that when remote viewing is used as a tool at the start of a search or during an investigation, some of the information could have been particularly helpful. Well done to a few of you, though I will say, there was one star among us, who offered not only one hit, but several."

"Can you at least give us the letter of *that* person?" Ed joked.

"I can," Allison said, right before taking a sip from her silver thermos. "It's D. Nice work, Devon."

CHAPTER TWENTY-TWO

A week and a half later, on the second to last Saturday in June, I sat at the kitchen table finishing an English essay I needed to turn in before junior year ended the following week. I squeezed my eyes tight, trying to block out the noise from the stops and starts of my neighbor's lawnmower, wishing time would speed up as I waited to find out if I had been accepted into the summer class at the station.

I bit down on my lip, planning some sort-of bullshit content to stretch my paper to a second page. I recalled the deal I made with myself: once I completed this task I could read Mom's journal again, some reward-system tactic I learned in school sophomore year for students who tended to procrastinate.

In the midst of wondering what I could write next, I thought of how Walter and Ed had high-fived me at the end of class, said I had "honestly impressed the hell out of them." How Gloria had given me her business card in case I had any further questions. How Bobby said he hoped to make it into the summer class too, and for me to keep in touch if neither of us did.

My phone buzzed.

I turned the phone over and read a text from Gwen saying "Hey" to both Frankie and me. She asked to get together for a mandatory meeting in the tree house in a half hour, if we were around. Frankie texted me privately:

**Told you G'd come to her senses. Meet me there
in five so we can gossip before she arrives.**

I texted Gwen **okay,** Frankie **see you in five,** and then shut down my laptop, hoping Gwen really had come to her senses. Most importantly, I hoped she forgave me for what I did—especially after I explained why in the letter.

I shut the slider door, feeling my muscles tense at the idea of meeting after what happened. Maybe Gwen would tell Frankie and me that she had gotten back with Andrew, that we needed to mind our own business, which, after the ups and downs of their relationship, honestly wasn't out of the question.

I stepped across the dry, scratchy overgrown grass in the backyard that Dad hadn't bothered to cut, while I squinted at the late afternoon sun peeking over the trees. Dad hadn't cut the lawn for weeks, since he spent pretty much every weekend now with Tina at some hemp festival or natural-food farm fair or whatever fake fun fest he went to these days.

Careful not to touch the splintered rungs, I climbed the wooden ladder, still unsure when might be the best time to tell Dad about Mom's journal. Secretly, I looked forward to telling him I found it—when I could tell him that I knew all about his behavior, beyond the things I already knew from all the gossip I heard about his cheating on my mother at the Alante employee cookouts over the years. Did anyone ever call him on his actions, tell him he was a jerk, tell him he shouldn't have, tell him to go home and be a better husband? Did anyone, inside or outside our family, ever stand up to my father?

I pulled my feet inside the entrance and crawled to the back of the tree house so I could sit in my regular spot. Watching the birds fly across the yard, I felt sort of bad, too, like guilty. I didn't want to hurt my dad too much with my findings. But at the same time, a way bigger part of me wanted to drop the journal like a bomb at his feet so it would sear his heart the way my mother's had been seared, years before she decided to commit suicide.

The tree house shook, Frankie scaling the ladder while holding a bag of Funyuns in his teeth. "K, I'm thinking we can't throw it in her face when she gets here," he said, settling into his usual space to my left. He pulled his long legs in a crossed position and held out the bag of Funyuns. "Like saying we told you so, you know what I mean?"

"Who knows what she's even going to say," I said. I took a few of the salty treats from the half-empty bag. "She could have taken him back for all we know. I think we need to be open to anything, since neither of us has been in 'love.' We kind of have no clue."

"If that's what love is, then I'm all set," Frankie said, wiping his greasy hands on the leg of his shorts. "I'd rather stay with my hook-ups, one of which I'm hoping to see tonight at McDougal's pool party, which I won't even bother asking you to go to since I know the answer now that you got your fill of the party scene for a while. Enough about Gwen, though, how did your last Super Sleuth class go?"

I shrugged my shoulders to my ears, pulled my knees into my chest. "Good. Really good, actually. I'm hoping to hear in the next few days whether I made the summer course."

"There's a sentence I never thought I'd hear you say—you wanting to go to summer school. I'm proud of you, D. Are you thinking you might want to study criminal justice at Massasoit Community or something, now that we're only a week from becoming actual seniors?"

I pushed a strand of hair out of my face. "No. I don't see myself going to college. In a perfect world, I'd love to do part-time work for the station, if that's even a thing, and then maybe work part-time for Alante's I guess. At least that way I'd get a decent paycheck. If I worked for the police part-time, I wouldn't mind as much having to work for my dad. How about you? What are you thinking about studying?"

Frankie stretched out his stick-like legs across the braided rug. "I heard psychology might be easy as a major, so I can party at the same time and still get good grades. Janice said maybe if I did mental health, she could get me into the hospital as a case worker or something."

I flinched back in feigned surprise. "Really? Wow. Frankie the therapist, who'd a thought?"

"Why not?" he asked. He ran a hand through his freshly washed hair. "Maybe my destiny, unlike yours, Nancy Drew, is to live an unassuming, quiet life in a nice, quiet neighborhood, you know, just like we have on Timber Lane."

Gwen laughed out loud below and then slowly stepped up each rung on the ladder. "We haven't had a nice quiet neighborhood since you 'upgraded' your muffler."

"Hey there, miss MIA," Frankie said, scooting over so Gwen could crawl through. "I need to make sure it's really you, since we haven't seen you in so long."

Gwen scooted to the opposite side of Frankie, keeping her gaze to the floorboards once she got settled. "I know. I just needed some time, but I know you both knew that. You knew everything, really . . . like the fact that I had a total asshole for a first boyfriend." Gwen lifted her head to the ceiling, her eyes filling with tears. "Ugh, I can't even talk about the whole thing without wanting to cry."

I pulled on a loose thread in the worn rug, looked over at Frankie.

"I'm really okay," Gwen said, exhaling and shaking her hands to get herself together. "I'm just embarrassed and humiliated and sad and frustrated and lots of things at once, which is what my new therapist Rhonda encouraged me to tell you—all the basic feelings I'm experiencing. I have 'mental health' homework now, writing every day in my new journal. My parents said I had to get a therapist. Which of course was the second order of business after we filed a restraining order against he-who-will-not-be-named. Anyway, that's what I called this meeting for, to tell you guys how I feel about the whole thing, and to say thanks for being good friends. If we don't talk about it more than that, that would be awesome, okay?" She rested her chin on top of her knees.

"Well, then, you won't be needing Frankie's services," I said, trying to keep the situation light. "Since our boy said he's thinking of studying psychology in college."

Gwen looked at Frankie. "That's great. Good for you. Maybe I should think about that too, becoming a therapist who helps dumb teenage girls break up with loser, abusive boyfriends, since I have zero motivation these days for pre-med."

A weighted feeling fell over me, knowing how hard it was for Gwen to admit she might have been wrong about something, especially something as hard as this. A squirrel scampered across the roof. I thought of my mother, how she went back and forth between anger and love for my father. "Stop beating yourself up," I said, feeling compelled to say something to make Gwen feel better. "And stop calling yourself dumb or stupid or whatever else negative you're saying. You thought you were in love. Maybe you were in love. I don't know. Who am I to say?"

"That's just it," Gwen said, leaning over her legs. "I get confused whether it was love or it wasn't. My therapist said it's seventeen-year-old love, which works out in some cases but most often doesn't. I'd just like to think that it really was love, or at least started out as love, so I don't feel so bad."

A car drove past out front of my house on Kingston Road blaring loud rap music from their car radio. If my parents had broken up after high school, if their seventeen-year-old love hadn't lasted, would my mother still be alive? But then, would I have been born?

"Thanks for the letter," Gwen said to me, nudging me with her foot. "Amazing, really, the whole thing with your mother. That's crazy. On a separate note, I'm sure you nailed the detective class."

Frankie wiped his mouth with the back of his hand. "Let's just say, when I need advice of any kind about the future, I'm going to D for a reading."

I sat back straighter against the wooden wall. "And if I need counseling, I'll call you, if you do decide to become a social worker or whatever."

Gwen relaxed her shoulders. "Yeah, you would make a decent social worker, Frankie."

Frankie scratched the back of his head. "Having a father who left his wife and first-grade son to go start another family kind of qualifies me, don't you think? In the understanding dysfunction department, that is. I'm thinking that might be my college essay—how I've tried to not become my dad."

"You'd never be like your father," Gwen said, tightening her low ponytail.

"Thanks," Frankie said, looking up through his much-too-long bangs. "Just because our families do something doesn't mean we will too, right?"

"That'd be like saying that since Livvy had an eating disorder then I will," Gwen said.

"Or that I'd be a hothead like my father," I said, raising my brow.

"I don't know, dude," Frankie said, shaking his head. "You didn't see yourself going off on Gaston. You were all flailing and beating him on the back and whatnot. Admirable show, truly. And Gwen, I do have to call to your attention, in the bent of being a good case worker, that you have been a tad neurotic with eating these days." He imitated Gwen delicately picking up tiny pieces of food with his first two fingers and inserting them in his mouth.

"Shut up," Gwen said, kicking the side of Frankie's foot. "I've just been watching my figure. Give me one of those." She leaned over and grabbed a Funyun out of the bag.

"We could say, though," Frankie said, looking over at me, "that you might be like your mother in ways, who is totally getting her angel wings in heaven right now BTW, after sending you that dream about Gwen."

I felt lightness in my chest. I savored it for a moment, watching a blue jay fly across the darkening yard. "Maybe I am like her in ways, minus the drugs and alcohol part. I mean, she kept a journal like I do, even if it's filled with dysfunction I'm not quite ready to process yet." I laughed, purposely letting my friends know that I felt okay about it all and didn't need to talk about it more than that at the moment. I guess for the three of us, it wasn't exactly how we all wanted it to be, meaning our family lives and our social lives and stuff, but it was all still okay.

"Well, when you are ready to process, we're going to need another mandatory meeting," Frankie said. He pretended to raise a glass. "To our messed up family members and our not-so-perfect lives."

Gwen chuckled, closing her eyes. "Here here," she said, as we all raised fake glasses in the growing dusk.

Frankie's phone buzzed. After checking it, he sat up on his heels. "I'm glad you're good, G. I mean it. I got to get going though, need to freshen up for the ladies. All this talk on dysfunction . . . aren't teenagers supposed to be talking about what they're doing on a Saturday night?"

"If you're normal, then yeah," Gwen said, twirling her earring. Then she glared at Frankie, looking like she used to, as if a different thought came into her head, making me feel like things might almost be back to normal. "Please tell me you're not hooking up tonight with that Goth girl from Spanish. She is literally a pot head."

Frankie tied his shoelaces. "That Goth girl happens to be hot and may I gently remind you that pot is legal. Besides, I'm not in a relationship, I'm merely hooking up with hot girls."

Gwen paused for a second, then scoffed. "That's disgusting and I'm just saying, you could get a disease."

Frankie leaned over and tapped both Gwen and I on the tops of our heads. "Relax, we're not talking about *that* kind of hook-up. I'm still Frankie from the hood, self-proclaimed Momma's boy. You two doing anything tonight?"

Gwen sighed. "I'm not ready to venture out yet. If you want to come over and watch a movie, Dev, I'm game."

"Sure," I said, feeling relaxed in a way I realized I hadn't in a while. Especially since all I'd been thinking about is if the police department would decide to take me on as part of the advanced class. "I just have to finish an essay." I figured I could reread Mom's journal in the morning, since Dad wouldn't be home by then either.

After Gwen and Frankie both left, bantering like they used to as they made their way down the ladder, I stayed up in the tree house for a little while longer. Leaves of the oak trees rustled in the evening breeze, causing some of the leaves to brush against the sides of the tree house. Dad used to tease me when they'd protrude inside the slats, said they were dinosaur fingers reaching in to get me. I used to feel scared, but then he'd make me feel safe at the same time, pulling me closer to him in a bear hug.

The feeling swelled inside me that I needed to tell him about the journal. Soon.

I just need to know the right time.

Birds chirped in little chirps around me, the spaces in between their chatter showing they were winding down for the night. Moms getting their babies ready for baths and books and bedtime—that's what I used to imagine when I was young.

Staring up over my house into the bruised-night sky in search of the North star, I hoped that since the situation with Gwen was resolved, that my mother would come to me again in my dreams, guiding me when it was time to confront my father—and about anything else I might need help with one day.

Mr. Coleman's back porch light flipped on, casting a glow across my yard—his creepy evening ritual of feeding the feral cats. I blinked to stay focused on my thoughts. If I started doing more of this work someday, intuitive work with the police, would she be able to help me? Or was her job done?

My phone glowed in the dark. I glanced down beside my thigh. Instantly, my heart leapt into my throat: A text from Bobby.

I picked up my phone with both hands and read the following message:

> **Hey. Figured it'd be okay to text, since you texted me that night from the party . . . and since the reason I'm texting might make the rest of your weekend. You made the class. (I did too, in case you were wondering whether my skills were as proficient as yours, ha ha). Have a good night. See you this summer.**

THE END

ACKNOWLEDGMENTS

Rebecca McCarthy, my editor, who has been a consistent supporter of my characters and my message. Thank you for everything you've contributed to Devon, and before Devon.

Liz Costanza, dear friend and initial proof reader extraordinaire, Jody Amato for copy editing and consistent positive encouragement, Clarisa Marcee for proofreading the final layout, Janica Smith for publishing assistance and expertise, Liz Doyle, treasured friend, neighbor and back cover copy superhero, Joe Merrick for engineering the audiobooks and for all the positive feedback along the way, and Yvonne Parks who created the perfect cover. Purple it is.

Carl, for your passionate support of my characters, my creativity, my intentions, my heart. Nothing would be achieved without the foundation you provide for our family.

Lastly, for the dreams that continue to heal, guide, and inspire me. They are the breeze that lifts me higher.

Photography by Maura Longueil

Jill Sylvester is a writer, speaker, host of the "Trust Your Intuition" podcast and therapist in private practice. She lives with her family, including their sweet, social bulldog, on the South Shore of Massachusetts..

For more information about Jill or to sign up for her blog, visit jillsylvester.com.

@jill_sylvester

Awakening

In *Awakening*, the first book of the *Devon: Dream Agent* series, seventeen-year-old Devon Alante struggles with crippling dreams that have plagued her as far back as she can remember. It isn't until she hears a voice calling her name though, that she realizes the dreams are becoming reality.

Trust Your Intuition

Winner of the Nautilus Book Award, *Trust Your Intuition* provides 100 simple tips and techniques designed to teach you to harness the power of your intuition, find meaning in your suffering, transform anxious and depressed feelings, and emerge stronger and more powerful than ever.

www.ingramcontent.com/pod-product-compliance
Lightning Source LLC
Chambersburg PA
CBHW070442120726
47910CB00003B/886